P
IN THE SAND

Barbara Cartland

Barbara Cartland Ebooks Ltd

This edition © 2014

Copyright Cartland Promotions 1976

Book design by M-Y Books
m-ybooks.co.uk

The Barbara Cartland Eternal Collection

The Barbara Cartland Eternal Collection is the unique opportunity to collect all five hundred of the timeless beautiful romantic novels written by the world's most celebrated and enduring romantic author.

Named the Eternal Collection because Barbara's inspiring stories of pure love, just the same as love itself, the books will be published on the internet at the rate of four titles per month until all five hundred are available.

The Eternal Collection, classic pure romance available worldwide for all time .

THE LATE DAME BARBARA CARTLAND

Barbara Cartland, who sadly died in May 2000 at the grand age of ninety eight, remains one of the world's most famous romantic novelists. With worldwide sales of over one billion, her outstanding 723 books have been translated into thirty six different languages, to be enjoyed by readers of romance globally.

Writing her first book 'Jigsaw' at the age of 21, Barbara became an immediate bestseller. Building upon this initial success, she wrote continuously throughout her life, producing bestsellers for an astonishing 76 years. In addition to Barbara Cartland's legion of fans in the UK and across Europe, her books have always been immensely popular in the USA. In 1976 she achieved the unprecedented feat of having books at numbers 1 & 2 in the prestigious B. Dalton Bookseller bestsellers list.

Although she is often referred to as the 'Queen of Romance', Barbara Cartland also wrote several historical biographies, six autobiographies and numerous theatrical plays as well as books on life, love, health and cookery. Becoming one of Britain's most popular media personalities and dressed in her trademark pink, Barbara spoke on radio and television about social and political issues, as well as making many public appearances.

In 1991 she became a Dame of the Order of the British Empire for her contribution to literature and her work for humanitarian and charitable causes.

Known for her glamour, style, and vitality Barbara Cartland became a legend in her own lifetime. Best remembered for her wonderful romantic novels and loved by millions of readers worldwide, her books remain treasured for their heroic heroes, plucky heroines and traditional values. But above all, it was Barbara Cartland's overriding belief in the positive power of love to help, heal and improve the quality of life for everyone that made her truly unique.

AUTHOR'S NOTE

Jane Digby, grand-daughter of the first Earl of Leicester, is one of the most fascinating women in history.

For descriptions of her exploits in search of love I am deeply indebted to her biography in Lesley Blanch's delightful book *The Wilder Shores of Love* and E. M. Oddie's *Portrait of Ianthe*.

The details of Bedouin life are all from diaries of the period written by Lady Ann Blunt and J. L. Burckhardt.

Jane Digby El Mezrab died when she was seventy-four, still beautiful and still deeply in love with her Sheikh.

Sir Richard Burton translated his celebrated and successful *The Arabian Nights* after he was tragically forced to leave Damascus by the Foreign Office, who never appreciated his brilliant qualities.

All other life is living death,
a world where none but phantoms dwell.
A breath, a wind, a sound, a voice,
a tinkling of the camel-bell –

Chapter One
1870

"Oh, no, Papa! I could not possibly marry Lord Bantham!"

Vita spoke decisively but her father, General Sir George Ashford, replied,

"I daresay his proposal has come as a surprise to you, Vita, but I assure you that your mother and I consider him to be a most suitable husband.

"But he is *old*, Papa! He is your friend! I never thought he was even interested in me."

"Bantham has a dignity and reserve that is very much lacking in many of the young men of today," the General replied loftily. "In modern parlance he does not wear his heart on his sleeve. And what is more he loves you and wants you as his wife."

"It's quite ridiculous! He is far too old!"

Even as Vita spoke she realised that she had made a mistake – for her father had been forty-five when she was born and Lord Bantham was only just forty.

At the same time the idea genuinely appalled her.

She had every intention of getting married sometime and there were already a number of attractive men who had laid their hearts at her feet.

The fact that most of them had been dismissed by her father as fortune-hunters did not perturb her.

At eighteen she told herself, as she refused suitor after suitor, there was plenty of time.

It was not surprising that she was in no hurry to be married, for Vita was so beautiful that she turned the head of almost every man she came into contact with.

Her features were perfect in her small face, her red-gold hair waved round an oval forehead and her deep-blue eyes with their long dark lashes looked violet when she was angry or upset. Her skin was very white with a wild-rose flush on the cheeks.

But what men found even more alluring was the fact that she was so radiantly animated that it was difficult to be in her company for more than a few minutes without being fascinated and entranced.

No name could have been more appropriate than the one that had been given her by her father at her birth.

He had expected a boy, for like all English fathers he was confident that his first child would be a son and heir.

But Lady Ashford had nearly lost her life in bringing Vita into the world and in fact at one moment the doctor informed Sir George that it might be impossible to save either the child or her mother.

When finally the General looked down at his daughter, half-suffocated and an ugly colour because of it, it was with an expression of relief because not only the baby but also her mother was alive.

"A girl, Sir George!" the doctor had said in an over hearty voice, well aware that the doctor was usually blamed when the expected heir was not forthcoming.

"So I see!" the General had remarked dryly.

"I wonder what you will call her?" the doctor asked. "'She was certainly determined to live although the odds were against her."

"Then she must obviously be named Vita!" the General replied with a flash of the wit he was famous for in his Clubs.

He and his wife had already chosen a number of family names for the expected son.

The fact that the baby was a girl had taken them by surprise and, when Lady Ashford was strong enough, she protested volubly against her husband's choice.

But with that streak of determination that was to carry him to high rank in the Army, he had persisted in saying she was already named!

By the time the Christening came Lady Ashford had added Hermione, Alice and Helena to her daughter's name, but Vita was the first.

Vita she remained and every year the name became her better.

Standing in the drawing room of the Ashfords' house in Leicestershire, Vita looked exceedingly lovely despite the fact that her eyes were stormy as they were raised to her father's face.

He had spoilt her all her life, but she was well aware of his obstinacy, which she often found echoed in herself. She knew now that he had made up his mind that she should marry Lord Bantham and it was going to be very difficult not to obey him.

In most things, as her mother had said often enough, Vita could twist her father round her little finger, but at times, especially when he had convinced himself that it was for her own good, he could be surprisingly determined.

She could not imagine how she had not realised sooner that Lord Bantham was interested in her.

She supposed that it was because he was so obviously her father's friend that she had not noticed the usual signs by which she sensed a man was about to declare himself, long before he did so.

She did not have to listen to what her father was saying now to know that Lord Bantham was a matrimonial catch.

In the Society in which the Ashfords moved an unmarried girl was a source of endless speculation and manoeuvring until she was safely embarked on the matrimonial sea.

The fact that she was not only beautiful but also rich had given Vita a very good idea of her own worth long before she left the schoolroom.

It was doubtful if she had ever been really secluded in her schoolroom and isolated from the Social world.

As she was a superb rider, she had been allowed to hunt since she was eight and, because she was dashing, impetuous and completely without fear, she was the pet of the very smart and exclusive hunts that were to be found in Leicestershire.

Her father had always been an outstanding horseman and it amused him in the absence of a son to take his small daughter out hunting with him and to find at the end of the day that she was 'in at the kill'.

One freedom led to another and by the time she was fifteen Vita was more sophisticated and more self-assured than any of her contemporaries.

Because she had a child-like appearance with her small boned figure, her wide-apart eyes and her tiny aquiline nose, she was flattered, cosseted and spoilt by everyone she came into contact with.

It was only when at seventeen she was officially 'out' that the women looked at her askance, realising that they had little chance when it came to competing with anyone so exquisite.

Vita was far too intelligent not to realise that her father and her mother were extremely nervous about the men who pursued her.

They were determined that she should marry a man they both approved of and who they felt would protect her from the many dangers that must await anyone so beautiful.

That they should have finally chosen Lord Bantham appalled her, while at the same time she was honest enough to admit there were some good reasons for their decision.

Lord Bantham was one of the richest men in England and he was also very distinguished.

He was not to be found amongst the gossiping Social sets whose extravagance and frivolity were said to shock Her Majesty the Queen deeply.

He was a pillar of the House of Lords.

And owing to his knowledge of country life he had been offered, and had accepted, the Presidency of almost every committee, association and organisation concerned with the preservation of rural England, and his houses and estates were without parallel in the whole length and breadth of the land.

As a matrimonial *parti* there was in fact no one to equal him, but as a man –

Vita shuddered.

She looked again at the firm line of her father's chin.

Sir George had been arrestingly good-looking when he was young and even now he was an exceedingly handsome man.

She glanced at her mother and saw the apprehensive and apologetic expression on her face, which told Vita all too clearly that her mother would support her husband's decision and she would receive no help there.

'I have to be clever about this,' she told herself.

"Bantham will give you everything that you will ever need in life," her father was saying. "You will be one of the foremost hostesses in London, as he has always wanted someone to entertain for him politically. Apart from that his racing stud is unparalleled!"

This was something that he knew would appeal to his daughter.

The General had a few horses in training, but he concentrated mostly on hunters to carry him and Vita during the winter season.

That was not to say that he did not enjoy racing. Vita had often accompanied him to Newmarket and to Epsom, and last year, when she was officially 'out', she had attended Ascot in the Royal Enclosure,

There had been no doubt that on the green lawns, thronged by the cream of Society, she had attracted nearly as much attention as the horses themselves.

Lord Bantham had won the Gold Cup and the General, having backed the winner heavily, had been delighted.

They had gone to congratulate Lord Bantham, and in retrospect Vita could remember that he had held her hand longer than was strictly necessary.

But all men did that when they had the chance, and all men, looking into her eyes, found themselves lost for words or even stammered a little.

Lord Bantham had not done that.

In fact Vita was unable to recall anything except that he had seemed rather duller than usual.

There were many of her father's friends who were raffish, gay and amusing. They flirted with her ardently, teased her with a glint in their eyes and flattered her outrageously.

But Lord Bantham had merely looked at her and she had been far too busy with those who were more eloquent even to notice him.

"The Bantham diamonds are magnificent!" Lady Ashford said suddenly. "I remember seeing his Lordship's mother wearing them at one of the Court balls. She seemed to be literally covered in diamonds! They even excelled those worn by the Queen herself!"

"Vita does not need many jewels at the moment," the General said, "but, of course, as she grows older she will find they are a great adjunct to a woman's beauty."

They were pressing her, Vita thought, pushing her into a corner from where she would find it difficult to escape.

With difficulty she forced a beguiling smile to her lips.

"You have taken me by surprise, Papa!" she said. "You must let me think about it further. There is so much I want you to tell me – so much to explain."

She knew that this was an appeal her father would find irresistible and immediately the determined look on his face gave way to one of tenderness.

He put his arm round her shoulders and pulled her against him.

"You know, my dearest," he said, "all I want is your happiness and for you to take your rightful place in the Social world."

He looked towards his wife before he continued,

"We are getting old, your mother and I, and it worries us in case we should die and leave you alone and unprotected."

He gave a little sigh.

"Apart from anything else you are a very rich young woman. I often wish your Godmother had not been so generous!"

"So no one could accuse Lord Bantham of being a fortune-hunter!" Lady Ashford added.

She had a manner of stating the obvious, which her husband often found irritating.

Now he did not reply, but bent to kiss his daughter's forehead.

"As you suggest, Vita, we will talk about it later."

"Thank you, Papa."

Vita stood on tiptoe to kiss his cheek and then with a smile at her mother, she ran from the room with an ethereal grace that made it hard for anyone to realise that she was in fact grown up.

She went upstairs to her bedroom and closing the door stood for a moment staring ahead of her, her eyes violet and stormy, her lips pressed together.

How could this have happened?

How could it have been sprung upon her out of the blue so that she was as unprepared as if an anarchist's bomb had exploded at her feet?

"I will not marry him! *I will not!*" she cried.

Without meaning to she spoke aloud, so that her voice seemed to come back at her from the four walls.

She moved towards the mantelpiece to drag at the bell-pull so violently that within a few seconds a maid came running, an anxious expression on her face.

"What be the matter, Miss Vita?"

"My riding clothes – quickly! And order a horse – no, I will go to the stables myself! Just help me change!"

The maid unfastened her dress at the back.

"Where is Martha?" Vita asked.

"Downstairs, 'aving a cup of tea, miss. She wouldn't 'ave expected that you'd 'ave wished to change so early.

"I am aware of that!"

She had a sudden longing for Martha, who had been her Nanny since she was a child and who she always turned to in time of trouble.

But Martha was set in her ways and this was the hour when she had her cup of tea in the housekeeper's room.

There would be no hurrying her back to duty until the last drop was finished.

Emily, who waited on Vita and for that matter on Martha also, helped her young mistress into a riding habit of dark green velvet that accentuated the beauty of her skin and brought out the red lights in her gold hair.

Impatiently, hardly looking at herself in the mirror, Vita put her high-crowned hat with its soft gauze veil on her head and, picking up her whip and riding gloves, hurried from the bedroom down the back stairs so that she would avoid encountering her father.

If she did meet him, it was quite likely that the General would wish to accompany her and insist on her waiting until he was ready to do so.

He did not like her to go riding alone, which Vita was well aware of.

But, having reached the stables and ordered one of her favourite horses to be saddled, she refused the suggestion that a groom should accompany her.

"I am only going in the Park for a little exercise.

"If you asks me, miss, you're a-missin' the exercise you takes on an 'ard day's 'unting!" the Head Groom said with the jovial familiarity of an old retainer.

"I am indeed, Headlam!" Vita agreed. "And that is why I must not become lazy nor must the horses."

"I'll see to that, miss," Headlam said with a grin.

He helped Vita into the saddle and watched her appreciatively as she rode off, managing the skittish overfresh stallion with a skill that made him say to himself as he had said thousands of times before,

'Aye, she be a chip off the old block!'

Away from the stables and on the soft grass of the Park, Vita gave her horse its head.

After galloping at a speed that brought the colour to her cheeks and allowed several golden curls to flutter round her forehead, she turned her horse in the direction of a long low house that lay sheltered by some trees in the centre of her father's estate.

She rode towards it, but, before she reached the gate, a man came riding from it and when they met there was no mistaking the gladness and admiration in his eyes.

"I was looking out for you," he said, "but I did not expect you so early."

"I meant to come after luncheon," Vita said, "but something has happened and I had to see you!"

There was a note in her voice that made him glance at her sharply.

He was a nice-looking young man, slim and wiry and he was clearly a gentleman by birth. But he had neither the polish nor the elegance of the men who clustered around Vita in Mayfair drawing rooms or who partnered her at the balls where she was invariably the belle.

Charles Fenton was in fact the son of the agent.

His father had served with Sir George and, when they had both left the Army, the General had asked Major Fenton, a valued member of his staff, to look after his estate.

It was something he had never regretted, for Major Fenton was an excellent manager and had made it his life's work to improve the Ashford properties.

It was inevitable that Vita would come in contact with Charles and that he would fall in love with her.

She accepted it as a matter of course but, while she was fond of Charles, she did not treat him seriously as an admirer for the simple reason that she knew that in the circumstances he could never be a suitor for her hand.

The difference in their positions and the fact that Vita was an heiress in her own right made it impossible for him even to contemplate the idea of her becoming his wife.

But, because he was grateful for the crumbs that fell from the rich man's table, Charles thought himself honoured and privileged to be her friend,

"What has happened?" he asked now.

"Papa wants me to marry Lord Bantham!"

"Lord Bantham?" Charles ejaculated. "But he is old – old enough to be your father!"

"I know that. They are thinking of making me safe, of shutting me up in a cage – a prison!"

Vita spoke violently.

"What are you going to do?" Charles enquired. "Have you told your father that you have no wish to marry anyone so old or so dull?"

"I started to say so," Vita replied, "but then I realised that Papa had made up his mind. You know what he is like when he gets obstinate."

Charles Fenton nodded.

They were walking their horses side by side and his eyes were on Vita's lovely face.

"You could not marry a man unless you loved him," he said and there was a depth in his voice that she did not miss.

"No, but what can I say to Papa?"

"Can you not plead with him?" Charles asked, thinking how hard it would be for anyone to resist Vita if she pleaded or begged a favour.

She was silent for a moment and she then said,

"I am only eighteen. Even if Papa does not physically propel me to the altar, he could make it extremely difficult for me if I refuse to do as he wishes."

"How?" Charles enquired.

"Last year, when Papa was annoyed about a certain, young man whom he forbade in the house, I refused at first to agree not to see him again."

"What happened?" Charles asked, conscious of a stab of jealousy that Vita should have wished to see any man, whoever he might be.

"Papa threatened me!" Vita replied.

She saw the expression on Charles's face and laughed.

"Not with violence!" she said. "Papa would never lay a finger on me. Neither he nor Mama even smacked me when I was a child. He had more subtle punishments."

"Such as what?" Charles asked.

"For one thing, he said he would forbid me to ride unless I agreed to what he wanted."

Vita gave a sigh.

"Can you imagine what I would suffer if I could not go near the horses, if the grooms were ordered to keep me out of the stables?"

"It would be sheer cruelty!" Charles agreed hotly.

"And there are other things Papa can do," Vita continued. "He has the handling of my money. He could prevent me having any new gowns or going to London. He even threatened once to send me to stay with my great-aunt Edith who lives in Somerset!"

"You must not go away!"

"If I stay I shall have to do as Papa – wishes," Vita said in a low voice, almost as if she spoke to herself.

She drew in her breath.

Then she said,

"You know what it is, Charles? They think, because I look like Cousin Jane, I might behave like her and the result is they are ensuring that is exactly what I shall do!"

"Cousin Jane?" Charles queried. "Which is she amongst your many relations?"

"We have talked about her before," Vita said impatiently, "Jane Digby. She has had four husbands and so many lovers that everyone has lost count of them! She is now married to an Arab Sheikh!"

"Oh, Lady Ellenborough!" Charles Fenton exclaimed.

"Lord Ellenborough was her first husband," Vita said, "and, now I think of it, he was exactly like Lord Bantham! Important, rich, distinguished – and I have always been told that the Digbys hustled their daughter into marriage when she was seventeen simply because she was so beautiful. They were afraid for her and I am certain that Mama and Papa are afraid now."

She was silent for a moment and then she said,

"I think it must have been William Steele, who made them decide I should get married.

"Who is William Steele?" Charles asked and his voice was cold.

"Oh, merely a rather attractive rake," Vita replied lightly. "He is looking for an heiress, but, because he is so handsome and so elegant, it is fashionable for all the girls to pretend they are in love with him. It amused me to take him away from them, but I was never serious."

She paused.

"But someone whispered poison about William into Papa's ears and he made the most ridiculous fuss!"

"And that is why he has decided you must marry Lord Bantham?" Charles asked. "Oh, Vita, if only you were not so lovely, so incredibly beautiful!"

Vita gave him a smile that was calculated to make any young man's reason turn upside down.

"Thank you, Charles!" she said, "but at the moment it is more of a liability. How can I escape from Lord Bantham?"

"You will have to think of something," Charles said gloomily,

"I know that," Vita replied.

Then she exclaimed with a note of anger in her voice,

"How can they be so stupid, so absurd as to follow exactly the same pattern that brought Cousin Jane so much suffering and so much unhappiness?"

Charles did not answer and she went on,

"She ran away with Prince Felix Schwarzenberg because she loved him – but she never loved Lord Ellenborough and that was why her first marriage was – so unhappy."

"I think a woman would be unhappy with any man if she does not love him," Charles remarked.

"You tell that to Papa!" Vita exclaimed. "But you are right, Charles, it is what I have always thought myself and I have been determined, absolutely determined, not to marry a man unless I find him completely irresistible, unless I am sure that I cannot live without him!"

"Could you not ask Lord Bantham to leave you alone?" Charles suggested.

"Do you suppose that would do any good?" Vita asked scornfully, "He thinks he is doing me a favour. After all, he must have been pursued for years by women who wanted to wear the Bantham diamonds or to sit listening to his prosy speeches in the House of Lords!"

"He has some fine horses!" Charles commented,

"That is the only redeeming feature about him!" Vita exclaimed. "But I would be marrying him – not his horses!"

She gave a deep sigh.

"Do you suppose, if Cousin Jane had known what was going to happen in her life, she would have run away from home rather than marry Lord Ellenborough? Oh, dear, I wish I could ask her!"

"Does she not live in Syria?" Charles asked.

"She lives with her Arab Sheikh in the desert and they also have a house in Damascus," Vita answered, "When Bevil Ashford, another cousin, was here a month ago he told me all about her."

"Is he not a diplomat?"

"Yes, Bevil is spoken of as being 'very promising', according to the family. He has made his mark in Russia, in Norway and in Syria, which was where he met Cousin Jane."

"What did he say about her?"

"He said she was beautiful. Still beautiful at sixty-two! She will be sixty-three this year!"

"That is amazing when you think of the life she has lived."

"Perhaps love keeps her young.

"She cannot still be in love at that age?" Charles exclaimed.

"That shows how little you know!" Vita retorted. "Bevil said that she is really in love with her Sheikh, just as

I gather that she was in love with two of her other husbands, with her two Royal lovers, both Kings, and with innumerable other men!"

"You can hardly want to be like that!" Charles said in a shocked voice.

"Cousin Jane has always been held up before me as an awful example!" Vita said. "The family talk of her with bated breath. In fact they talk of little else! News of Jane brings all my aunts, great-aunts, cousins, first cousins, second cousins and third cousins together like a flight of parrots. They sit there talking and talking, chewing over every scandal that Cousin Jane has ever been embroiled in."

Vita gave a gay laugh before she added,

"The thing that makes them raving mad is the fact that she is still beautiful and still happy!"

She looked at Charles and said,

"You resent it too. Is it not extraordinary? Nobody can really bear it that a woman who has sinned is not in sackcloth and ashes, weeping her eyes out, so that they can be magnanimous and forgive her. But Cousin Jane does not want to be forgiven!"

"How do you know?"

"Well, she caused a tremendous commotion when she came to England thirteen years ago. The family gathered round her, but it was out of curiosity and not affection."

"Why did she come?"

"I think she must have felt an urge to come back to where she belonged and then found, when she did, that 'home is where the heart is'," Vita replied. "And her heart is in Syria."

"It all sounds very strange to me.

"I was too young to be taken to meet her," Vita said wistfully. "She was fifty, but everyone who saw her had to admit that she looked beautiful and after she left they talked of nothing else."

She smiled.

"As the years passed they used to say, 'do be careful in front of the child'. But as I grew older I pieced Cousin Jane's story together like a jigsaw puzzle. Now, helped by Bevil, I have learned a great deal more about her."

"I cannot think why you should be interested," Charles said stiffly. "Your family is right, Vita. No normal woman would marry an Arab and want to live in the desert."

"I think it sounds very exciting!"

"If you were there and saw it for yourself, you would find it sordid, uncomfortable and doubtless, at times, very dangerous!"

"It *is* dangerous!" Vita said. "Bevil told me that. But it must be thrilling ruling over a Bedouin tribe and being free of the snobbish jealousies and Social strivings that exist in England."

She paused then added,

"And not having to marry someone one dislikes – like Lord Bantham!"

"You don't have to marry him," Charles said. "No one, not even your legal Guardian, can force you to say 'I will' when the moment comes in the marriage ceremony!"

Vita's eyes shone.

"It would be amusing to wait until the Parson actually says, 'Wilt thou take this man to thy lawful wedded husband?' and then to say 'no'!"

"You could not cause such a commotion, a scandal in Church!" Charles exclaimed.

"Could I not?" Vita asked, "I can do anything I want to do."

"But you must not want to," he said with a caressing note in his voice. "You are too lovely, Vita, too perfect in every way, to have everyone speaking about you unkindly."

He paused and then said in a low voice,

"You know all I want is for you to be happy. I would lay down my life if I thought it would help you, but I am powerless."

Vita smiled at him.

"You are very kind, Charles, and you know how much I rely on you and trust you. You must help me – I cannot – do this."

"How can I help you?" Charles asked desperately.

Vita did not answer and after a moment he said,

"I cannot believe that you would consent to run away with me – but if you would, there is no need for me to tell you what it would mean to me."

"Dear Charles!" Vita said. "I don't think that that would solve anything. They would catch up with us eventually and the only result would be that Papa would sack your father and then we would never be able to see each other again."

"Then how can I help you?" Charles asked despairingly.

"It is a comfort for me to talk to you, to know that you are on my side. Everyone, as you know full well, will say, 'your father knows best'. 'You must do as your father wishes'. 'How can a girl of eighteen know her own mind?'"

"But you *do* know," Charles quizzed her.

"Of course I do," Vita replied, "and I get more and more convinced every moment that passes that I would not marry Lord Bantham if he were the last man on earth!"

She paused and then said,

"Have you ever looked at his hands, Charles? He has short rather stubby fingers. I know I could never bear him to – touch me."

"Vita, don't talk like that!" Charles pleaded.

Now there was an edge to his voice and unconsciously he spurred his horse so that it moved forward suddenly.

It was a moment or two before Vita caught up with him.

"Have I made you unhappy, Charles?" she asked.

"You always make me unhappy," he answered. "It is like looking up in the sky and seeing a star that is so beautiful, so desirable that you know your life is empty if you cannot own it and yet knowing with despair that it is utterly and completely out of reach."

"Oh, Charles, how poetic!" Vita exclaimed.

She looked at him with her large eyes and then she said,

"If I loved you, I would run away with you. We would go somewhere where no one could find us. An island, perhaps, far away where we would be blissfully happy just being together."

"But you don't love me!" Charles said in a hard voice.

"I love being with you and talking to you," Vita said, "but that is not enough, is it?"

"No," he replied. "It is not enough for you, and I don't think, eventually, it would he enough for me either!"

"What is love like, Charles?" Vita asked.

He gave a short laugh before he said,

"Do you really want me to tell you?"

"I am asking you as a friend."

"I cannot tell you as a friend." he answered. "For a man who loves you, it is an agony and an ecstasy. It is a pain that strikes through one's whole body and mind until one can handy bear it another moment! Then suddenly it is a rapture that sweeps one up into the sky and one knows that, after all, the pain is worth it!"

There was a throb in Charles's voice as he spoke and, after a moment, Vita said very softly,

"Thank you, Charles. That is what I must find – one day."

"I don't like to think about you feeling like that for some other man," Charles said. "At the same time I could not bear you, of all people, to accept what is inferior or imitation. You are entitled to the best, Vita!"

"That is what I feel myself," Vita said. "Life should be an adventure, Charles, a very exciting adventure, if one is not shut up in a gilded cage and loaded with diamonds to keep one quiet!"

"You will have to be careful what you do and what you say," Charles warned. "The most important thing is to play for time."

"Why?" Vita asked.

"Because once you are married it will be too late!" he answered. "And I have the feeling that, while a long engagement might suit you, Lord Bantham will be impatient."

"Why should you think that?"

"Because any man who wanted you would be afraid of losing you," Charles said savagely. "He would be inhuman or blind, deaf and dumb, if he did not realise that every man you meet is likely to fall in love with you and you might easily prefer someone else to him."

"I would prefer anyone to him!" Vita interposed.

"I expect he is too puffed up with his own importance to think that likely at the moment," Charles said. "At the same time he might brook no delay and your father might agree."

"You mean Papa might anticipate I would run away if he realised how antagonistic I am to the idea of marrying Lord Bantham?"

"Make no mistake, Vita," Charles said, "the General is a very clever and astute man. My father has always had a great respect for him. He has often told me what a magnificent Commander he was and how the men would follow him anywhere."

"I am sure of that," Vita said.

"Equally," Charles went on, "he had something of a reputation as a martinet. It was he who gave the orders and he who insisted on their being carried out. I have a feeling that he may be just as authoritative when it comes to your marriage."

"You are right, Charles!" Vita agreed. "And all because he thinks it is 'for my own good'. Oh, how I hate that expression!"

"Perhaps I am wrong and it is!" Charles said.

"After what you have said to me about love?" Vita asked. "You cannot back out of it now. You have incited me to rebellion and you must stand by the consequences."

"Vita, don't do anything rash!" Charles begged her apprehensively.

He knew how impulsive she was and he knew too that she had her father's autocratic way of expecting the world to be there for her to walk on.

"I have a feeling," she said, "that an idea will come to me – an idea of how I can escape. Help me, Charles! What can I do? How can I play for time, as you suggest?"

They rode for a little while in silence before Charles said,

"Have you no relatives that you could talk to? I don't mean your cousins living round the corner, I mean someone in Scotland or France. What about your cousin Bevil? Where has he been posted?"

"He is on his way to Mexico," Vita said. "He is only paying a visit to the country, so that is hopeless!"

She gave a sudden cry,

"What is it?" he asked.

"You have solved it! Oh, Charles, you have solved it for me! You have told me what to do and I shall always be eternally grateful!"

"*I* have solved, it?" Charles asked in bewilderment. "But I thought you said that you could not go to your Cousin Bevil?"

"Not Bevil." Vita answered, "but to Cousin Jane! That is where I will go! I told you I wished I could ask her advice – she is the only person who will understand."

"She is in Syria!" Charles said. "You cannot possibly go to Syria, nor do I think your father would allow you to stay with someone who has behaved as Lady Ellenborough has done!"

Vita laughed and it was a sound of pure amusement.

"Dearest Charles, I am not as stupid as that!" she said. "Of course I shall not tell Papa I am going to Cousin Jane. You will be the only person who will know that! But that is exactly where I am going and no one – but *no one* is going to stop me!"

*

Two hours later Vita walked into the study where her father was sitting in front of the fire reading a newspaper.

He looked up when she appeared and thought, because it was impossible to think anything else, how lovely his daughter looked.

Wearing a demure white gown, which, however, revealed her softly curved breasts and small waist, Vita might have stepped out of a picture by Gainsborough and, as if she had deliberately intended to inspire such a thought, she carried a pink carnation in her hand.

Her skin was very white and with its wild-rose colouring she looked the perfection of good health as she crossed the room.

Yet there was something very fragile and ethereal about her that aroused in every man she met a protective instinct, until they looked at the dancing light, which was somehow provocative, in her blue eyes.

Vita reached her father's chair and bending over kissed him affectionately on the cheek.

"I have brought you a carnation for your buttonhole, Papa," she said. "It will make you look even smarter and more dashing than you do already!"

As she spoke, she slipped the carnation into his lapel and then kissed him again before she sank down on the floor beside his chair.

"I feel better now, Papa," she said. "I went riding and it has made me think more clearly and more sensibly than I did when you spoke to me about marrying Lord Bantham."

"I am glad about that, my dearest," the General said, "but I wish you had asked me to go with you. You know I don't like you riding alone."

"I kept to the Park, Papa, and I wanted to think."

"And what conclusions have you come to?"

"I came to the conclusion that I have the most wonderful, kind, adorable father in the whole world," she said slowly.

The General smiled appreciatively. At the same time there was a slightly wary expression on his face.

"I have a feeling. Vita," he said, "that you are trying to get something out of me. If you are trying to make me say that you need not marry Lord Bantham, you are wasting your time."

"I am leaving such a difficult and rather frightening problem in your hands, Papa," Vita said in a child-like voice. "If you really think that he will make me happy, then I must comply with your wishes."

"That is exactly what I hoped you would say," the General answered. "You are being very sensible, my dearest, and I promise you that you will never regret trusting me in this matter."

"I am sure of that, Papa. But, if I agree to your plans, I will you spoil me a little first?"

The General looked at his daughter and there was a twinkle in his eyes as he said,

"I felt there was something behind your compliance! What do you want?"

Vita knelt so that her arms were on his knees and her eyes in her small pointed face were looking up at him.

"You said something to me once. Papa," she said, "that I have never forgotten."

"What was that?" he asked.

"You said that no one could be considered an educated or indeed civilised person until they had visited Italy."

"Did I say that?" the General enquired. "Oh, well, perhaps I did! It is, after all, what I think. It is a very beautiful country and I have always been sorry that your mother and I have been unable to take you there."

"I think, before I marry, I should go to Rome and perhaps Naples," Vita said.

"So that is what you are trying to inveigle me into promising?" the General exclaimed.

"Is it too much to ask, Papa? It would be so wonderful to see the Coliseum in Rome and Pompeii. I have a feeling that Lord Bantham is so busy that we will not have much time for travelling."

"Nor have I at the moment," the General said. "You know as well as I do, Vita, that my new appointment as High Sheriff of the County makes it impossible for me to go abroad for at least two months and there is a great deal to be done on the estate."

"Italy would not be the same without you, Papa, to explain everything to me," Vita said. "At the same time I feel it would be very good for my education, which you have said often enough does not finish because one is grown up. There are plenty of people who would chaperone me – Lady Crowen, for one."

The General did not reply and Vita went on,

"I know she is an old gossip, but her husband was a diplomat and she has travelled a great deal. Besides, she speaks Italian."

"When did you think up this little scheme?" the General asked.

"I have been thinking about it for a long time," Vita answered. "In fact I have actually discussed it with Lady Crowen and she has given me one or two lessons in Italian. It was to be a surprise when you and I set off for Italy!"

The General did not speak and Vita moved until she was half-sitting on his knees with her arms round his neck.

"Please, darling Papa, let me go to Italy," she begged. "Once I am married I shall have to settle down and do everything my husband wants me to do. I may even have a baby and then it might be difficult for me to travel and you have always made me enjoy it so much!"

It was true that the General had taken Vita to France and Brussels and Denmark on different occasions.

They had even planned at one time to visit Hungary, because the General was so anxious to buy some horses he had heard glowing accounts about.

Instead they had gone to Ireland and had come home with two hunters, which had been the envy of the whole neighbourhood.

"I must think about it," the General said at length.

"Please, Papa, you know how insistent you have always been that I should be well-educated. You have always said how much you hate stupid women and I feel that there is just a little blank spot in me that would be filled in if I saw the Forum, the Leaning Tower of Pisa and the excavations at Herculaneum."

She drew his head down nearer to hers as she spoke.

She was very soft and sweet in his arms and she smelt of roses.

Quite suddenly the General capitulated.

"Have it your own way," he said and kissed her cheek.

"You mean – I may go?" Vita cried. "Oh, darling, wonderful Papa, I do love you!"

Chapter Two

Vita stood on the balcony of her bedroom and looked out over the Bay of Naples,

The blue of the sea, the distant hills and the tiny fishing villages clustered down beside the breaking waves were so beautiful that she drew in her breath.

With a sense of elation she realised that she had won!

She had reached Naples and now the real adventure that she had set her heart on was about to begin.

Everything had gone far more smoothly than she had anticipated.

Once her father had made up his mind that she should go to Italy before she married, he was impatient to get the journey over.

She guessed that he half regretted his promise and she suspected that Lord Bantham had something to do with this.

But the General was a man of his word and, having told Vita she could visit Rome and Pompeii, he was not going to disappoint her.

Only to Charles had Vita dared to admit that the ideas she had in mind were not confined to absorbing culture.

"It will be quite easy, Charles," she told him, "to find a ship that will take me from Naples to Beirut, which I think is the nearest Port to Damascus."

"You will have to persuade Lady Crowen to accompany you," Charles replied. "Supposing she refuses?"

"I shall manage somehow," Vita said vaguely.

Charles had looked at her sharply.

"You are not thinking of doing anything stupid like going alone?" he asked. "If I thought you would do that, I swear I would go to the General here and now and tell him what you are contemplating."

"If you were so treacherous and so mean, I would never speak to you again, Charles!"

"Which would be better than my brooding over all the dangers that you might encounter if you did something crazy on your own," he retorted. "After all, Vita, your life has always been very sheltered. Abroad you have had your father to protect you."

Vita did not answer and he added,

"Promise me, swear to me by all you hold holy, that you will do nothing which might involve you in serious trouble."

"What do you call serious trouble?" Vita enquired.

"You are too beautiful and far too young to travel about the world without an army of soldiers to guard you!"

Vita laughed.

"What fun that would be! But I cannot imagine the War Office agreeing to supply me with troops of my own!"

Charles had pleaded, remonstrated and argued with her, but, when Vita had actually left, he had the unsatisfactory and extremely painful impression that she would do exactly what she wanted to do.

And that was what she had intended from the very first.

It was Vita who had thought that they should start their journey from Naples rather than travel through France and Italy to Rome first.

"It will be quicker and far more comfortable to go straight to Naples by sea," she had said to her father. "I am always frightened when we travel by train that my luggage will be lost or we will end up at the wrong place. It will not be the same without you, dearest Papa!"

"You will have a most efficient Courier," the General replied. "I have known Davenport for years and he will see to your luggage and everything else. All you will have to do is enjoy yourself."

He had, however, conceded that it might be best to do as Vita suggested and travel by ship to Naples.

Vita thought secretly that he had decided that this was a way of getting her home more quickly and therefore he was quite prepared to agree to it.

They had set out from Tilbury in one of the newest and most up to date P. & O. Steamships, which were scheduled to reach Bombay in twenty-five days, a considerable improvement on previous years.

The General had seen them off and, after he had held Vita in his arms and kissed her several times, he had said to Lady Crowen with a deep note of concern in his voice,

"You will take care of her?"

"You know I will, Sir George!"

Lady Crowen was, as Vita had anticipated, so delighted to be going to Italy that she would have agreed to anything the General suggested. But she was in fact very fond of Vita and extremely grateful to her for having asked for her chaperonage.

The Courier, Mr. Edward Davenport, was a middle-aged man with grey hair and a quiet courteous manner that endeared him to all his clients.

He was very much in demand amongst Senior Army Officers because, when he undertook to escort their children or their wives to obscure parts of the globe, he always managed it with great competence and made himself so pleasant that those he had looked after always declared that he was indispensable.

Vita would have found him rather dull were it not that on the second day of the voyage she found that he knew Syria quite well and she managed to make him tell her many facts that she had previously been ignorant about.

She had no wish to make him suspicious of the motive of her questions and she was clever enough to base all she wanted to know on the fact that her particular interest lay in Arab horses.

As it happened, the General had explained to Vita many years ago the significance of the strain of Godolphin Arabian and Darby Arabian in the English thoroughbred stock. So she already knew quite a lot about the Arab mares that they were descended from.

Mr. Davenport talked to her about the Bint El Ahwaya breed belonging to the children of Ishmael from which all the real Arab horses were descended and it was easy to mention quite casually her cousin, the Honourable Jane Digby El Mezrab, as Bevil had told Vita that she was now known as in Syria.

There was a pause and Vita knew that Edward Davenport was feeling embarrassed and wondering how he should speak to her of the woman who he well knew had shocked all her family.

But Vita had been prepared for this.

"You must not feel shy of talking of Cousin Jane to me," she said. "Another cousin, Bevil Ashford, has talked of her so much, but of course not in front of Papa, that I feel I already know her."

"I am afraid that your cousin has lived a somewhat controversial life, Miss Vita," Mr. Davenport said uncomfortably, "and, as you can imagine, even in Syria her marriage to a Moslem and a Sheikh has given rise to a great deal of criticism."

"Yes, of course, I know that," Vita said, "but I understand that Sheikh Abdul Medjuel El Mezrab is in fact an Arab Nobleman."

"That is true," Mr. Davenport agreed. "His blood is as blue as that of his wife. In fact, among his own people it was even considered that his marriage was a *mésalliance*, but naturally no one would think that in England."

"Tell me about Cousin Jane," Vita begged him.

But Mr. Davenport was too afraid of the General to be indiscreet.

"She is very beautiful," he said briefly.

Vita found it impossible to get much more out of him. She did, however, by keeping on the subject of horses, learn a little about the Arab tribes and, as Bevil had told her, that the desert could be a dangerous place.

"The desert Arabs are in a permanent state of warfare," Mr. Davenport said. "Plundering and skirmishing are for them an everyday pastime."

He saw that Vita was listening attentively and went on,

"The two great rival tribes are the Shammer and the Aeneze. Your cousin's husband is, of course, a Sheikh of a branch belonging to the Aeneze."

"Do they hate each other? " Vita enquired.

"There are centuries of blood feuds behind them," Mr. Davenport replied, "and for one tribe to venture into the territory of the other is often a matter of life or death!"

Then, as if he felt that he had made it sound too bloodthirsty, he went on,

"But it is not always as dramatic as that! Some Bedouins are really brigands and they have worked out a way in which they can fleece the unwary traveller in a most unscrupulous manner."

"What is that?" Vita enquired.

"It happened to me once," Mr. Davenport confessed. "I was travelling in a caravan with some sightseers when a band of robbers, they were nothing less, swept down upon us with a terrifying display of horsemanship and, of course, the firing of flintlocks and the brandishing of spears!"

"Were you terrified?" Vita asked curiously.

"It was unpleasant," Mr. Davenport admitted, "but I had a feeling that our lives were safe, if nothing else."

"What happened?" Vita enquired.

"They took everything they could lay their hands on. Then suddenly at a given moment there was the dramatic appearance of another band of horsemen."

"Who were they?" Vita asked.

"All part of the same tribe" Mr. Davenport replied. "They appeared to drive away the first lot and defeat them and then claimed a reward for saving our lives!"

Vita laughed.

"So you paid twice? "

"But of course!" Mr. Davenport said. "That was the idea of the whole performance!"

To Vita it all sounded fascinating and it made her more determined than ever that somehow she would get to Syria.

The idea had been further cemented in her mind before she left England when Lord Bantham called to bid her farewell.

He had obviously been told by the General that Vita had accepted his proposal of marriage and there was, she thought, a self-satisfied look of triumph in his eyes and a somewhat unpleasant smile on his thin lips.

"We will be married a month after you return from abroad," he said. "The Prince of Wales and Princess Alexandra have graciously intimated to me that they would wish to be present at the Marriage Ceremony."

"How very satisfactory for you!" Vita said with a touch of sarcasm in her voice.

Then, as if she realised that she had been indiscreet, she said quickly,

"I know I shall find it nerve-wracking to have a very large wedding with such important guests!"

"There is no need to be frightened," Lord Bantham said pompously. "I will tell you what to do and see that you make no mistakes."

"That will be very kind of you," Vita said in what she hoped was a grateful tone.

They were alone in the drawing room and Lord Bantham put out his hand to take hers.

"I feel sure that we shall be extremely happy together," he said, "I have a great deal to teach you and I am sure that you will be a willing pupil."

"Yes – of course," Vita replied.

She spoke in an amenable childlike voice, but found it hard not to shudder because Lord Bantham was holding her hand.

She could see his thick stubby fingers and she could feel the strength of them on hers.

She had a wild desire to snatch her hand away.

Then she was aware as his arm went round her that Lord Bantham intended to kiss her.

Only just in time did she turn her face so that his lips touched her cheek and not her mouth, but even that was enough to make her feel a revulsion and a horror that was almost as intense as if she had touched a reptile.

She knew then that he revolted her and that she had indeed been right when she had told Charles that she would not marry him if he was the last man on earth!

With a little twist of her body she extracted herself from his arms.

"I think Papa is waiting to see you," she said. "There are so many things he wishes to discuss and we must not keep him waiting."

"There is no hurry," Lord Bantham protested.

There was a note in his voice that told Vita all too clearly that she must keep out of his reach.

Quickly she pulled open the door and it was impossible for him to touch her again in the sight of the footmen on duty in the hall.

After that Vita took the greatest care never to be alone with Lord Bantham.

She realised, on several occasions before leaving England, that he was manoeuvring so that they could be alone, but she always managed to circumvent him.

She thought that he was a little nonplussed by her attitude, but she hoped that he put it down to her youth and inexperience and was too complacent to suspect an ulterior motive.

Lord Bantham had in fact suggested that he should travel with them to Tilbury and see Vita off as her father intended to do.

She had, however, also managed to avoid the embarrassment of a train journey and the fear that he might insist on kissing her before she left.

"I want to be alone with you, Papa," she said to the General. "It would be such a bore to have someone else present when you know that there are still thousands of questions that I want to ask you about Italy. It would not be the same to have a stranger listening."

"Lord Bantham is hardly a stranger, my dearest," the General replied automatically.

At the same time he was flattered that Vita wished to have him to herself and so he had given in to her demands.

'Lord Bantham is horrible! I will never marry him!' Vita told herself as the ship left the shores of England and it was a refrain that she reiterated a thousand times on the voyage.

At the same time she was so busy planning what lay ahead that it was easy to ignore the menace Lord Bantham would prove if she returned to England without a solution to her problem.

Every day that carried her further away from the man her father had chosen for her made her more and more sure that she was right in deciding against a marriage that would inevitably prove as disastrous as her cousin Jane's had been with Lord Ellenborough.

It was impossible not to think with pleasurable anticipation of Jane and her wild, colourful and sensational life.

It was Bevil who had set the picture for Vita by saying that Jane was a romantic adventuress and what she was seeking was love – real love, which she was certain was waiting for her somewhere in the world if only she could find it.

"You really believe that she has found love with her Sheikh?" Vita asked.

"It took her some time," Bevil said with a smile. "She certainly enjoyed a great number of heartthrobs before finally she reached the East and found the man she now calls her 'dear and adored one'."

"Tell me about the loves that failed her," Vita begged, but Bevil bad shaken his head.

"You are far too young and much too inquisitive! If your father and mother knew that I had even mentioned Jane to you, I should be thrown out of the house."

"You are not the only person who talks about her," Vita pointed out.

It was true that she already had a vivid picture of Jane's life.

There were plenty of people to relate with relish how unhappy and broken-hearted she had been when her lover, Prince Felix Schwarzenberg, had deserted her the very moment that her divorce from Lord Ellenborough was granted by the House of Lords.

Left broken-hearted and with two children, someone of less strength of character might have collapsed, but in quite a short space of time the family learnt that Jane was in Bavaria, the mistress of King Ludwig, with whom she had fallen head-over-heels in love.

The King was a cultured, charming and somewhat eccentric man, who was known to be irresistibly attracted by beautiful women.

Jane had lived in Munich and was at first extremely happy.

The King had fired her with an enthusiasm for sculpture and painting and engendered in her a love of Greece that was to find fulfilment when King Ludwig's son, Otto, became King of the Hellenes.

Before this happened Jane unexpectedly married Baron Carl-Theodore von Venningen, a Bavarian Nobleman.

This was only possible because King Ludwig had personally intervened with the Vatican to allow the Baron, who was a staunch Catholic, to marry a divorcee.

Why this marriage had been a failure Vita could never find out.

Jane's letters to her relatives at home had apparently not been very revealing.

What they did learn, to their horror, was that a Greek, the most handsome and attractive man in the whole country, Count Spyridon Theotoky, had fallen in love with her.

There was the story of a terrible duel in which the Count had been shot in the chest and had only been nursed back to life by Jane herself.

On his recovery Jane had run away with him to Paris, once again fleeing from matrimony, respectability, husband and children.

There was a second divorce and the Theotokys had left Paris for a new home in Corfu.

"At last she has settled down!" Vita learnt that her aunts and great-aunts had said triumphantly. "Now let's pray that she will behave herself!"

Looking out over the Bay of Naples with its strange ethereal light that was different from anything Vita had ever seen before, she wondered if the atmosphere and beauty of the Mediterranean had anything to do with the restlessness that had made Jane, after fifteen years, break up yet another marriage.

Perhaps it was simply the irresistible fascination and charm of King Otto, to whom Count Spyridon had been appointed as an *aide-de-camp* or was there something wild and primitive in the atmosphere that made Greece seem different from the other parts of the world where Jane had lived.

Vita could understand her being swept away by the romantic idealism of a young King combined with all the classical beauty that remained of Greece's past glories.

And yet, once again not even a King was able to give her the love she sought.

There were whispers and here Vita had had to listen very attentively, because they were considered far too improper for her young ears, of an Albanian General.

"She said," one of the aunts quoted, "that he was a splendid man, very tall, handsome and as seductive at sixty as a man half his age!"

Vita could hear the sudden in-drawing of heavy breath before everyone's lips were pressed in a line of disapproval which belied the glint of excitement in their eyes.

"She was demented about him! They lived together in the mountains, galloping wildly on their rough horses during the day and sleeping in a camp surrounded by brigands – yes, brigands – at night!"

"She must have been crazy!"

"It was disgusting! Disgraceful! We should never have spoken to her again!"

But Vita knew that their disapproval was basically only in words.

In fact they longed to hear all about Jane, they wanted to talk about her, they wanted to learn even more than they knew already about her wild, intriguing, fantastic life. She made everything they did seem colourless and unimportant.

There was a French writer, a friend of one of the family, who had referred to some of the scandals about Jane when he had met her in Paris.

He admired her overwhelmingly and, when he met her again in Athens, he wrote home rhapsodising over her perfect figure, her chestnut golden hair, her aristocratic hands and feet, her large deep-blue eyes.

"*Her skin has that milky-whiteness that is so essentially English,*" he wrote. "*She colours at the slightest emotion and her passions may be seen agitating in their imprisonment.*"

This sort of language was extremely shocking, especially as it came from an outsider, but Vita felt that she could understand it and she knew it would have been to her a perfect ending to the tale if Jane had found happiness with her Albanian brigand.

But long before Vita was old enough to understand such behaviour, Jane had already left General Hadji Petros, the Chief of the Pellikares.

He had disillusioned her, as so many other men had managed to do and once again she believed herself to be heartbroken!

At forty-six she left Greece to visit Syria!

There, Vita learnt, she had finally found the real love she had been seeking all her life.

'What I want to ask her,' Vita told herself now, 'is whether all those men, all those unhappinesses, all those heartbreaks were worthwhile.'

She paused before continuing her question in her mind,

'If Jane had met her Sheikh when she was my age, would she ever have wanted another man, or would she have lived with him happily ever afterwards?'

It was a question, Vita knew, that only Jane herself could answer and that was why she was determined, with a strength of purpose that her father might have recognised as part of himself, to go to Syria.

And Fate seemed to be playing into her hands.

Before they arrived at Naples, Lady Crowen had been taken ill. It might have been caused by the somewhat turbulent passage through the Bay of Biscay, it might have been something she ate or perhaps, as Vita thought secretly, she was really too old to go adventuring.

Anyway, when they reached Port, she was carried from the ship, taken to the best hotel in Naples and put straight to bed.

The large suite that Edward Davenport had engaged for them was very comfortable and Vita had no compunction about leaving Lady Crowen to the ministrations of Martha while she went off to explore the City with their Courier.

She was not only interested in what she saw, she also wanted to take her bearings.

Because she was extremely intelligent and very astute when it came to getting her own way, it was quite easy after they had completed a tour of the City to tell Mr. Davenport that she thought she should return to the hotel to be with Lady Crowen.

Actually, on reaching the hotel, Vita immediately slipped out again through a side door and took a hired carriage to the nearest shipping office.

The clerk, a dark-eyed, susceptible Italian, who was bowled over by Vita's appearance, was prepared to lay the whole office and himself at her feet if he could be of service.

He soon told her everything she wanted to know.

Yes, there were ships leaving Naples almost every day and quite a number of them called at Beirut.

Yes, it would be possible for her to engage a most reliable Courier, who not only knew Syria but also spoke Arabic.

Vita arranged everything with the dark-eyed Romeo and he recommended a ship that was leaving the following morning, as being the most comfortable and the most suitable for anyone so lovely.

While Vita waited, he then produced the Courier, as if he was a magician bringing a rabbit from out of a hat, and Vita found him a pleasant man with exactly the qualities she required.

She had made up her mind that before she reached Syria she would learn some Arabic.

It was infuriating now to think that, although she knew four languages well, she had not even the vaguest idea of how to speak Arabic, which she was sure was really necessary on the journey she planned to undertake.

After all, as she had already learnt, it was seventy-two miles from Beirut to Damascus.

It was a dangerous road, where it would be essential for her to have someone, who not only understood the danger of marauding bands of brigands but who could also hire for her the caravan of horses and camels she would need.

The Courier told her his name was Dira and that he was in fact half-Arab.

He seemed to Vita to be a fairly well-educated man and, although she had no means of judging whether his Arabic was good or bad, he was at least fluent in it.

She told him that her desire to reach Damascus was in order to see her cousin, the Honourable Jane Digby El Mezrab, and that obviously impressed him quite considerably.

"The lady is very well known," he said, "and greatly respected. Her house is extremely fine!"

Vita thought that his voice held a note of awe in it and she remembered that Cousin Jane was wealthy which, she was sure, would be appreciated by the Arabs in Damascus.

She engaged Signor Dira and paid over the money the Italian clerk demanded for the tickets.

Then, having arranged to meet the Courier at the ship at seven o'clock the following morning, she went back to the hotel.

She had taken the first step in her grand adventure! But there was a great deal more to do.

She had to obtain money.

Although Vita had some money with her for what her father called her 'shopping expenses', the bulk of the money was for safe keeping in the hands of Mr. Davenport.

After thinking about the situation for some time, Vita decided that this was the moment when she must sell the jewellery she had brought with her for this very purpose at this particular moment in her travels.

It was obvious that she would have to ask difficult, if not embarrassing, questions, but finally she decided to enquire of the concierge in the hotel if it would be possible for someone in his office to take her to the best jeweller in Naples.

The concierge looked surprised at the request.

"Signor Davenport has this moment gone up to his room, *signorina*. If you need an escort, should he not take you?"

"No, no, he is tired. He has had a long day and besides I wish to surprise both him and the Contessa, who is, as you know, unwell."

This the concierge understood immediately.

Beguiled by Vita's baby-like expression and innocent blue eyes, he sent her off in a hired carriage with one of his staff to a jeweller who he assured her was the most honest in all Italy.

Vita rather questioned this. At the same time she found him very obliging.

The clerk in the main part of the shop showed her into a back room, where she explained to the proprietor how she wanted to give her kind friend, the Contessa, a large sum of ready money for her poor son who was in trouble, having incurred some heavy gambling debts.

"If I tell her I am about to sell my jewellery, she will not allow me to do so," Vita said, "and therefore I must do it behind her back. Once it is sold and I have given her the money, it will be too late for her to refuse my help."

"You are quite certain that the jewels are yours, *signorina*?" the jeweller asked a little suspiciously.

But his qualms were easily set at rest by the frankness in Vita's lovely eyes and the warmth with which she told of her desire to help the poor young man and his distracted mother.

"I am rich, *signore*," she said, "but that is my good luck – and I cannot be so heartless as to allow my friends to suffer."

"Your kind heart, *signorina*, does you great credit," the jeweller said approvingly.

Vita looked shy, but she did not try to bargain with him.

Finally he gave her a large sum of money, which was, she knew, only a little less than the jewels were actually worth.

She could not help thinking that perhaps someone else, who had not given the impression of being so trusting, might have fared far worse.

Now Vita had jumped her second fence and the only one that remained was to get away in the morning without anybody being aware that she was leaving the hotel.

Martha, having been extremely disagreeable for most of the trip, since she was getting old and really disliked travelling, had unpacked Vita's clothes, but fortunately had left her trunks in the lobby outside her bedroom.

Vita had no intention of taking all her clothes with her, only those she thought she would need in Damascus and especially her riding habits.

As soon as she was alone, she pulled a large valise into her bedroom and packed it quickly and skilfully with only the necessities she expected that she would need on the voyage and when she reached Cousin Jane.

She then sat down to write a letter to Lady Crowen.

She explained to her quite frankly that she wanted to see her cousin whom she had heard so much about ever since she was a child.

She was well aware that she would not have been allowed to visit her had she asked to do so, and she was therefore taking the law into her own hands and was journeying to Syria accompanied by a most competent Courier, who had been well recommended to look after her on the journey.

"I do not expect, dear Lady Crowen," she wrote,

"to be away for more than three weeks. Will you and Mr. Davenport wait here for me?

When I return, we will consider amongst ourselves what we shall say, if anything, to Papa. I beg of you not to write to him at the moment and upset him.

You know how busy he is and it would distress him quite unnecessarily if he learnt I had gone to Syria. I shall be back within twenty-one days – perhaps sooner. There are ships, I understand, calling almost every day at Beirut – "

She paused, looked down at what she had written and then added with an impish grin,

"Perhaps Mr. Davenport would be wise to buy back my jewellery, which I have sold to a very reputable jeweller whose address I enclose. I told him a sad story that I needed it for a young man who had lost a great deal of money gambling!

Mr. Davenport should say that the gambler has retrieved his losses and wants to reimburse me for the money I lent to him. We would not wish Papa to ask what has happened to my jewels when I return home – "

Once again Vita paused and then added,

"Please, please forgive me if I distress you by what I have done. I assure you it is not, as you might think, an irresponsible action, but one that concerns my whole future most deeply.

I have to see my cousin for very personal reasons and that is why I hope that your Ladyship will not be angry but give me instead your understanding and add to it your good wishes for my safe return."

Vita signed and sealed the letter, addressed it to Lady Crowen and propped it up on her dressing table.

Martha, she knew, would find it when she called her in the morning.

She could imagine there would be a terrible fuss and commotion when they found that she had disappeared.

But there would be nothing they could do about it and she was certain that they would wait and not write frantically to her father, knowing that he would inevitably blame them for not having looked after her better.

Vita had contemplated letting Martha into her secret and taking her with her, but Martha was not the stuff that adventurers are made of!

Although Martha adored Vita and had done so ever since she was a child, she also trembled when she realised how closely Vita resembled her beautiful and notorious cousin, Jane.

It was Martha who was always saying,

"Beauty is only skin deep!"

"It's not looks that count but what's behind them."

"You look into a mirror, but God looks into your soul!"

There was a note in Martha's voice as she repeated these old adages that told Vita her thoughts were activated by fear – fear that the child she loved could no longer be controlled as she had been when a baby, but was developing a very distinct personality of her own.

Because she was fond of her old maid, Vita found it hard to resist the impulse to go to her bedroom and tell her not to be worried.

But she knew that, if she did so, Martha would somehow prevent her escape, because Martha, above all things, was a snob.

That Vita should become a Peeress, that she should be entitled to attend the opening of Parliament and would doubtless in time be offered a post in the Household of Her Majesty the Queen, was to Martha the glittering zenith of Social achievement.

She admitted that she thought Lord Bantham was a trifle old, but that criticism was easily offset by the fact that he was still a fine upstanding man. He was so extremely wealthy and of such Social consequence that any other deficiency could simply be ignored.

"But, Martha, I want to fall in love!" Vita had said when they discussed her marriage.

"You'll fall in love after marriage," Martha replied complacently.

"But how can you be sure of that?" Vita enquired.

"Because, dearie, a husband is what every woman wants. His Lordship'll look after you. You'll sit at the head of his table, entertain his guests and, if God is willing, give him children to comfort him in his old age."

Vita had shivered.

She had felt again that revulsion that had seemed to seep through her body like poison when Lord Bantham had kissed her cheek.

She was not quite certain what happened when a man gave a woman a child, but where Lord Bantham was concerned she was quite certain it would be unpleasant and something she could never tolerate.

She had known, however, that it was no use talking to Martha and so she could not expect her assistance in escaping from a marriage that she heartily approved of.

That left Cousin Jane.

There was nobody else.

And Vita lay night after night in the bright brass bedstead on the Steamship, deciding that she must take the last stage of her journey from Naples to Damascus alone!

*

When she had finished writing her letter to Lady Crowen, Vita went back to bed.

Martha had already helped her undress and had tucked her in before she said goodnight.

"I'll call you at eight o'clock, dearie," she said, as she turned towards the door.

"Make it a little later, Martha," Vita replied. "I am tired tonight. I think I might sleep until eight-thirty or perhaps nine."

"Suppose you ring?" Martha suggested. "I've already arranged with the chambermaid that, if the bell of this room rings twice, she will fetch me immediately."

"That is a very good idea!" Vita agreed. "And I really am very tired. It must be the heat."

"You don't think you're sickening for anything?" Martha asked anxiously.

"No, of course not," Vita replied. "And tell Mr. Davenport that we will not leave for Pompeii until after eleven o'clock."

"I'll do that. Goodnight and God keep you," Martha said.

"Goodnight, dear Martha," Vita answered and lay back against the pillows until Martha had left the room.

She knew that this arrangement would give her a little more time to get away.

Although the boat was scheduled to sail at seven-thirty, there was every likelihood of its leaving late.

Vita had learnt already that the Italians were seldom on time.

They took life too easily to rush and bustle. They enjoyed themselves and in the City of Naples the Neapolitans were noted for their independence, for having minds of their own and for refusing to be subservient to any man.

This attitude unfortunately was difficult to live with, since it usually implied a certain amount of inefficiency and quite a lot of incivility.

But all Vita wanted was that the ship on which she was travelling should be free of the Port and moving into the waters of the Mediterranean before anyone discovered that she had left the hotel.

After that neither Lady Crowen, Edward Davenport nor Martha could do anything about it.

Her valise was packed and locked, her letter was written and now Vita walked to the window and pulled back the curtains.

Outside the stars were brilliant in the velvet of the sky.

Although there was no moon, they cast enough light to shimmer silver on the sea and all along the crescent shaped bay there were the lights gleaming from the windows of the small houses and climbing up the mountainside to shine like jewels in the darkness.

The air was warm and soft against Vita's cheeks and she suddenly felt a wild sense of excitement sweep over her.

For the first time in her life she was acting on her own initiative and doing something she wanted to do, without being constrained by parents, by Governesses, nurses and servants or even her own conscience.

She did not feel ashamed or apologetic for deceiving anyone.

She would never have contemplated behaving in such a manner if her father was not forcing her into marrying a man she actively disliked.

She had known from the very beginning that no amount of reasoning or logic would help her and that, however much she pleaded with him not to make her marry Lord Bantham, it would all have been a waste of time.

This marriage was what he thought was best for her and that argument was irrefutable. Nothing she could say or do could change his mind.

And yet to marry Lord Bantham, Vita thought now, would be worse than deliberately committing suicide.

It would destroy all her hope of happiness, all her dreams and her beliefs in everything that was spiritual and beautiful.

It was difficult to remember how old she had been when she first began to dream of the man she would love and who would one day love her.

But he had always been there, interwoven in her thoughts, a man who was different from all the men she had ever met, who possessed all the qualities she knew she wanted in the husband to whom she would belong absolutely.

Perhaps because she was so lovely, her Governesses had always felt that they must teach her about the beautiful things that existed in the world.

The Taj Mahal, which a man had built for the woman he loved, to the pictures of Botticelli. The poetry written by men who had loved and suffered and which made Vita long to be the inspiration for something so spiritual and so perfect.

When she was thirteen, she had read Lord Byron's poems simply because one Governess had said that she did not think she was old enough to do so.

She read Shelley and Keats and devoured every romantic novel that she could obtain by one means or another.

There were in fact few of them in her father's library, but there were always girlfriends who would lend her a book that they would say because they knew it was rather naughty, 'don't tell Mama'.

These were romances that their eyes grew misty over and they sighed because they felt it would be impossible for them ever to know a love, which in the traditions of the time usually ended on a deathbed with a loved one sobbing bitterly beside it.

Vita, however, was not interested in deathbeds.

She wanted to live and she thought to herself that, just as Cousin Jane had sought a perfect lover and found him, she could do the same.

She was not sure what she would feel when he drew her into his arms and kissed her, but of one thing she was completely and absolutely certain, it would not be what she felt when Lord Bantham touched her.

A number of men had kissed Vita's hand and whispered words of passion when they were dancing in a ballroom or walking sedately in a lantern-lit garden.

But she had never allowed herself to be kissed on the lips, because she had decided that was something she must keep for the man she loved and would marry.

Now she thought with a sense of despair that if she was not careful the only husband who would touch her lips, unless Cousin Jane could help her, would be Lord Bantham!

'*I hate him*!' she thought wildly.

Then she knew that somewhere beyond the darkness and the stars, somewhere in the world that existed beyond the movement of the shimmering waves, was a man who would love her as she longed to be loved.

She felt that she must make a pilgrimage towards him and perhaps he would make one towards her.

She felt that her whole being surged out with a cry for help that must transcend the confines of time and space.

'Come to me! Let me find you!' Vita pleaded within herself. 'Let me know love as it should be – the love that is part of all the beauty in the world – the sea – the stars – the sky and tomorrow the sun.'

She felt as if her voice rang out across the water as she waited, half-expecting an answer, but there was only the silence of the night and a feeling of emptiness.

'I am all alone!' Vita told herself.

It was very frightening!

Chapter Three

The ship was moving through the blue of the early morning sea, but rolling as it did so from the wind, which was blowing the waves into white crests.

Signor Dira remarked gloomily that he thought they would have a rough passage to Athens which was their first Port of call.

This information did not perturb Vita who was a good sailor. The turbulence of the Bay of Biscay had had no effect on her while nearly every other woman aboard the Steamship had been prostrate.

Now she stood at the rail watching Naples fade into the morning haze and said briskly,

"I think, *signore*, we must start my Arabic lessons right away. We have little time and I have a great deal to learn."

She knew, as they sat down in a place protected from the wind, that Signor Dira was none too confident that she would learn much before they reached Beirut, but Vita was optimistic.

She already spoke French, Spanish and Italian, as well as a little German.

It was not an achievement to be particularly proud of when she kept remembering that Cousin Jane was known to be proficient in nine languages!

However it was a start, and she knew as the hours passed that Signor Dira was extremely impressed by the quickness with which she picked up the words he taught her and remembered them correctly when he asked her to repeat them some time later.

It would have been hopeless to embark on learning Arabic writing, but Vita tried to think of all the ordinary everyday words and phrases she would need to use and to memorise them.

She learnt that Signor Dira had an Arab father and an Italian mother and that he had lived in Syria until he was eighteen, when his father died and they had then moved back to Naples.

Vita immediately plied him with questions about the Bedouins and he was able to give her an answer to most of the issues that intrigued her.

She learnt, which was reassuring, that the ferocity and bloodshed of the tribal wars that Bevil had so vividly described to her were not as devastating as they sounded.

The Bedouins were armed mostly with spears and very old horse-pistols, which, in most cases, were more noisy than dangerous and the tribes also had an arrangement of payment – *nak el dam* – for casualties.

"The fine for blood," Signor Dira explained, "varies with every tribe. If an Aeneze kills another Aeneze the price is fifty she-camels, one *deloul*, a camel fit for mounting, a mare, a black slave, a coat of mail and a gun."

"What happens if the defeated enemy does not pay up?" Vita asked.

Signor Dira looked shocked.

"It is a point of honour with the Arabs," he replied. "When a tribe owes another for death, either of a human or of animals, it is paid however long it may take."

"It sounds a very civilised method of warfare," Vita said with a smile.

"It certainly prevents a great deal of killing," Signor Dira agreed.

Vita, being of course particularly interested in the Bedouin women, asked Signor Dira about their marriage ceremonies and whether it was true that the women were treated by their husbands just as chattels.

Signor Dira considered the question before he said slowly,

"While a Bedouin girl remains unmarried, she enjoys more respect than a married woman, for a father thinks it an honour and a source of profit to possess a virgin in the family."

"And after she is married?" Vita asked him.

"Then she lives only to please her husband," Signor Dira replied simply.

It sounded to Vita rather a bleak existence, but she remembered that Bevil had told her that Cousin Jane had become the perfect Bedouin wife, adoring her husband and perfectly happy to be dominated by him as she had never been dominated by her other husbands or lovers.

"Usually Jane wears the blue cotton gown which is the ordinary dress of a Bedouin woman," Bevil had said, "and, when she is in the desert, she even goes barefoot."

Vita could hardly believe it when she remembered how her relations had described the fantastic jewels Cousin Jane had been given by King Ludwig and other men who had adored her.

They also talked incessantly of her remarkable elegance and extravagance, so that it seemed incredible to think of her as so deeply in love that she gloried in waiting on her Bedouin husband as obediently as a woman of his own race would have done.

Vita could not help feeling that Bevil exaggerated and thought that it would be most illuminating to see for herself.

Even now that she was safely out at sea she could hardly believe that she had really succeeded in her desire to visit her cousin and engage her help in solving her problems.

But it was a fact that the ship that was heaving under her feet was carrying her away from her chaperone and the Courier engaged by her father and she was, except for Signor Dira, entirely on her own!

It was indeed the wildest and most fascinating adventure she had ever imagined.

All through the day Vita made Signor Dira teach her Arabic words and sentences, only relaxing occasionally to ask him more questions about the Bedouins themselves and especially about their horses, of which she wished to learn everything he could tell her.

She knew that the one thing that might mitigate her father's anger at the way she was behaving was if she could bring him back really interesting and instructive information about the Arabian thoroughbreds he was always so interested in.

Signor Dira was able to tell her a great deal she had not known before.

He told her that the tribe he belonged to owned many horses and one of his greatest pleasures in life was to ride.

"I am sure that my cousin, the Honourable Jane Digby, has some fine horses," Vita said.

"She has indeed!" Signor Dira replied. "Sheikh Abdul Medjuel El Mezrab breeds and buys only the best Arab horses for his tribe and his wife rides a mare that is the envy of all Damascus!"

He went on to explain that a pure-bred Bedouin thoroughbred usually stands from fourteen to fifteen hands in height.

"I understand," Signor Dira said, "that the head of an Arabian is larger in proportion to that of an English thoroughbred."

"My father always says that an Arabian's ears are usually fine and beautifully shaped," Vita remarked.

"That is true," he smiled, "and the tail is carried high, both walking and galloping. It is a sign of breeding."

When they had been talking about horses for some time, Vita remembered that when she held come on board at Naples she had seen a horse being lowered down into the hold.

She had not paid a great deal of attention to it at the time, because she had been so agitated that the ship might not sail or that Lady Crowen would discover she was missing from the hotel and have her followed.

But now, as they left Athens and the sea seemed even rougher than it had been, during the day, she said to Signor Dira,

"There is a horse on board. I wonder if it's an Arabian?"

"It is indeed!" he replied. "I was looking at it before you arrived. It is a stallion of the Sheyfi."

"What is that?" Vita asked.

"They are Arabians now existing only in the Royal stables in Italy," Signor Dira answered. "They are descended directly from Bint El Ahway and bred by the Kehilans who were known amongst the first followers of the Prophet."

"Tell me more," Vita quizzed him excitedly.

"The Sheyfi are very fine thoroughbreds and the only tribe who could have their stallions belong to Sheikh Shaalan El Hassein, a branch of the Shammer.

"The enemies of the Aeneze," Vita said quickly.

"Yes, that is right," Signor Dira agreed.

"I must see the horse on board," Vita said.

"He is a fine animal," Signor Dira told her. "I learnt that he has been sent to the Royal stables to serve the mares that are kept exclusively for the King's use."

"Let's go below and see him immediately!" Vita suggested.

She felt annoyed that she had wasted so much time already in forgetting the horse that she had noted vaguely, but she had been too beset by her own problems to realise what an opportunity it was.

There seemed to be no one of whom they could ask permission to go below and so Signor Dira, who knew his way about the Steamships that plied the Mediterranean carrying both passengers and cargo, helped Vita down the narrow ladders.

There was a smell of oil and bilge and it was certainly none too clean, but Vita had learnt that the Steamship she was travelling on was larger than most of those that called at Beirut and it was also faster.

There were few comforts, despite the glowing recommendations of the shipping clerk, and her cabin was furnished very sparsely. She suspected that she would find the mattress on her bunk hard and uncomfortable.

But everything was immaterial beside the fact that she was doing what she wanted to do and going where she wanted to go.

Now, moving somewhat unsteadily in the bowels of the ship, she thought how shocked her mother would be if she realised where she was at this particular moment.

They reached the stern and found the horse was in a roughly constructed stall, looking at them with large dark eyes.

He was a beautiful bay with black points, over fifteen hands high with large pointed ears. He had two white feet and a blaze down his nose.

"He is magnificent!" Vita exclaimed.

Signor Dira patted the stallion's neck, and after a moment Vita touched his nose gently.

"You need not be afraid," Signor Dira said. "All Arabians are gentle and affectionate. They have no fear of man and will allow anyone to come up to them when they are grazing and take them by the head."

"I had no idea of that," Vita said.

"Their extreme gentleness and courage is partly inherited and partly due to the fact that Arabians never have cause to learn fear," he explained.

Signor Dira smiled as he continued,

"They can often be a nuisance as they rub themselves against their masters and follow even the children around, so that it is hard to get rid of them!"

"How fascinating!" Vita cried.

The stallion nuzzled his nose against her while she talked to him, and she felt he liked being made a fuss of.

Then she looked at the uncomfortable stall he was housed in and said in consternation,

"Look, he has no water? And I cannot see any food!"

"No, that is true!" Signor Dira agreed. "I saw a Bedouin come aboard with him and there was also an attendant whom I thought was Italian."

"Do find out where they are," Vita said. "I am sure that the horse must be thirsty and hungry if he has been all day without attention."

Signor Dira obeyed her suggestion and Vita remained with the stallion. Carefully she noted and memorised his good points, thinking how exciting it would be to tell her father that she had actually seen a Sheyfi.

She was quite certain that if the stallion had been selected for the King's stables every point about him must be perfect and she knew that in comparison she would not make a mistake in admiring any inferior Arabians she might see while she was in Syria,

It was some time before Signor Dira returned.

He looked serious as he explained,

"'The Bedouin who is in charge of the horse is smitten with seasickness. I found him with some difficulty. He refuses to move or do anything except groan!"

"And the other man?" Vita asked.

"He has been sent in attendance from the Royal stables, but neither is he in a fit state to look after a horse."

"What do you mean by that?" Vita asked.

"Quite frankly, *signorina*, he is drinking. He also dislikes the sea and he has solved his sickness problem by drinking himself almost incapable!"

"How disgraceful!" Vita exclaimed, "You would think that whoever owns such a magnificent stallion would take more care of him!"

"I imagine Sheikh Shaa-lan will not be pleased at his servants' behaviour," Signor Dira said dryly, "but he is not here to see what is happening."

"Well then, we must look after the horse," Vita said. "Where can we find a pail?"

Signor Dira looked at her in surprise and said,

"I think, *signorina*, we should not interfere. Besides, this is not the sort of work that you should concern yourself with."

"I am always concerned with anything that affects an animal," Vita replied, "if you believe I could eat my own dinner and think of this horse thirsty and hungry, you are very much mistaken!"

She saw a faint smile on Signor Dira's lips and was quite certain that he was thinking of her as one of those crazy English who fussed more over their animals than they did over their children. But she was not concerned about that.

Asserting her authority, she insisted that he should find a wooden pail and fill it with water and, after searching around, she discovered a bag thrown down beside the horse's stall, which contained his food.

There was no doubt that the stallion was thirsty.

He drank the whole pailful of water and Vita sent Signor Dira, by now somewhat resentful, to refill it.

She fed the stallion and, when finally she was satisfied that he was as comfortable as it was possible to be on the heaving ship, she returned to the upper deck.

Over dinner, which was not very appetising, Signor Dira recovered from his irritation at being made to wait on a horse and expanded as Vita asked him more about Syria.

She flattered him by saying how grateful she was for the benefit of his knowledge and experience.

He had made it clear at the beginning that it was going to be an expensive affair to travel from Beirut to Damascus.

They would require protection from the bandits and brigands who preyed upon travellers, and Vita had already said that she wanted the best horses so that they would not be too long on the journey.

She was well aware that, the longer she was away from Naples, the more agitated and even hysterical Lady Crowen would become. Only by returning as quickly as possible could Vita prevent her from taking some drastic action about her disappearance.

It was a relief to know that, while they had to spend a night on board, they would arrive in Beirut early in the morning and Signor Dira was quite confident that he could obtain immediately good fast horses and an escort to take them to Damascus.

Vita could not help being amused when she realised that he was much more apprehensive than she was concerning dangers they might encounter on the journey.

Because she hoped that he would not decide at the last moment to return to Italy rather than accompany her, she tried to talk of other things.

"Tell me about a Bedouin marriage," she begged, knowing now that Signor Dira liked the sound of his own voice.

"Most of the Bedouins content themselves with one wife," he replied. "The ceremony is very simple."

"What happens?" Vita asked.

"Usually five or six days after *talab* – the betrothal – the bridegroom comes with a lamb in his arms to the tent of the bride's father and cuts its throat before witnesses. As soon as the blood falls to the ground, the marriage ceremony is regarded as complete."

"Surely they have a feast?" Vita enquired.

"They do indeed. A great deal of feasting and singing."

He paused, then after a moment, went on as if he chose his words carefully,

"Soon after sunset the bridegroom retires to a tent pitched for him some distance from the main camp. There he shuts himself up and waits for the arrival of his bride."

Vita smiled.

"I should have thought that it would have been the other way around."

"No indeed," he answered. "The bride, bashful and shy, runs from one tent to another until she is caught by the rest of the tribe and escorted in triumph by the women to the bridegroom's tent."

"Is she really so reluctant?"

"She is expected to scream and struggle," Signor Dira replied, "because that is considered maidenly and modest. Sometimes she fights so desperately that her husband even has to beat her into submission!"

Vita thought this sounded very primitive, but she did not say so.

As soon as dinner was finished, she thanked Signor Dira for all his kindness and retired to bed.

The sea was subsiding a little and she found it easy to undress without being tossed about.

Her last thoughts before she went to sleep were of the horse down below.

If he had not been fed and watered, he would now be suffering and she thought how angry her father would be if one of his horses had been so neglected by a groom.

Vita planned that, if there was time, she would slip below the next morning and see the stallion again before they arrived in Beirut.

*

But she slept late and only just had time to dress and be ready before Signor Dira knocked on her cabin door to tell her that the ship was coming into Port.

She hurried up on deck and gasped at the beauty of the mountains high above the small town.

The sunshine was brilliant and it made their peaks, still capped with the winter snows, seem dazzling.

There was almond and peach blossom on the trees growing down to the water's edge and the City with its square white houses and flat roofs looked, in Vita's eyes, very alluring and Eastern after the spires and domes of Naples.

"I wonder if the horse is all right?" she asked Signor Dira, as he joined her at the rail and the ship nosed its way nearer to the quay.

"I imagine his groom will have recovered by now," he replied.

"I think we should speak to him and tell him how badly he has behaved," Vita said. "The least he could have done if he was incapable, himself, was to ask someone else to see to the horse. Besides, if he had any sense, he would have put some water ready in the pail before the ship sailed."

"I do not think it would be wise for me to rebuke a servant of Sheikh Shaa-lan," Signor Dira said nervously.

"You sound as if you are afraid of the Sheikh," Vita said provocatively.

"He is very important, *signorina*.

"I still think one of us should speak to the man," Vita argued. "Otherwise he will do this sort of thing again and might really damage a fine and valuable horse."

Signor Dira did not answer and she knew full well that he was very reluctant to interfere in what he was quite convinced was not his business.

She thought too that he was perhaps nervous of starting a vendetta against himself with a Bedouin tribe.

At the same time it infuriated her to think that anyone could treat such an animal so negligently, and she was quite certain that if the journey had lasted even longer the Bedouin would still have wallowed in his seasickness and made no effort about the horse he was in charge of.

She was aware that Signor Dira standing beside her was debating whether he would do better to lose face where she was concerned by refusing to reprimand the groom or to incur the wrath of the Sheikh by interfering.

Then, as the ship came alongside the quay, he gave an exclamation.

"All is well, *signorina*," he said quickly. "There is no need for you to worry any further about the stallion."

"Why not?" Vita enquired.

"I can see Sheikh Shaa-lan," he replied. "He is here himself, so you can be quite certain that from now on the horse will have every attention."

"Where is he?" Vita asked.

In answer he pointed to where, standing a little apart from the crowds waiting on the quay for the arrival of the ship, there was an Arab dressed in a conventional white *kombar* or long gown.

Over it there was a black *abbas* embroidered with gold, which made him stand out as a person of high rank.

He wore the yellow boots that were greatly admired by the Bedouins and the conventional four cords of knotted camel hair on his head over a white *keffie*.

As they drew closer, Vita could see that he had a huge jewelled knife stuck in his belt and, when she was near enough to see his face, she saw that even without such trappings of authority she would have known that he was someone of high rank.

The Sheikh seemed a little taller than the other men moving round him and he also held his head with a proud imperiousness that gave him an air of authority that was unmistakable.

"So that is Sheikh Shaa-lan El Hassein!" she said almost beneath her breath, pronouncing the words in the way Signor Dira had taught her was correct.

"It is, *signorina*. But he is an enemy, a bitter enemy, remember, of Sheikh Medjuel El Mezrab and his wife!"

Vita looked at him with even more curiosity. Then, as the ship tied up alongside, Signor Dira hurried her away so that they could collect their belongings and be one of the first to step down the gangway.

A porter was found for Vita's valise and, as she stepped ashore, she was aware of a babble of sound unlike anything she had ever heard before.

She wished now that she knew more Arabic so that she could understand what was being said, but there was also a sprinkling of French amongst the words that met her ears.

"This way, if you please, *signorina*," Signor Dira said, giving his orders to the porter and ostentatiously clearing a path for Vita amongst the milling crowds.

Moving in the direction he wished her to go, suddenly she was aware that she was almost level with the Sheikh.

He was still standing somewhat detached from everyone else, although there were some Arabs near him, each wearing a black *abbas*. This made Vita think they were part of his tribe since the Aenezes, she had learnt, never wore black.

Quite suddenly she made up her mind and walked towards him.

As she did so, she was conscious that he was perhaps one of the best-looking men she had ever seen.

His features were classical although his nose was slightly higher-bridged than she might have expected of an Arab.

His eyes were dark, almost black, and she thought as she faced him that they were completely impassive and without a glint of interest in them.

"You are Sheikh Shaa-lan El Hassein?" she asked.

He looked at her sharply when she spoke and inclined his head.

"Do you speak French, *monsieur*?"

"*Oui, mademoiselle*."

"Then I wish to tell you," Vita said, "that the man you sent to look after the stallion, which was put on board this ship at Naples, is a disgrace! You should not allow anyone so untrustworthy to be in charge of such a fine animal!"

Because she felt so strongly about the treatment of the stallion, Vita spoke positively, almost aggressively and now she saw the Sheikh's eyes flicker over her almost insolently before he replied,

"Are you suggesting, *mademoiselle*, that my man ill-treated the horse?"

"Because he was seasick, he left the animal without water or food," Vita replied, "and, if I and my Courier had not fed and watered the stallion, he would undoubtedly have suffered on such a rough voyage."

There was a moment's pause and then the Sheikh asked,

"Can I believe this to be the truth?"

"Do you think, *monsieur*, I would have any point in informing you of this if I was not concerned for the animal in question?" Vita asked angrily. "The groom was seasick,

I am not denying that, but he should have made arrangements for someone else to see to the horse before the ship left Naples."

There was silence for a moment and then the Sheikh said coldly,

"I have noted what you have told me."

There was something in his aloof attitude that Vita found extremely irritating.

"Let us hope that you will be more careful in future, *monsieur*," she said and her voice was sharp. "In England we value our horses too much to allow them to be treated badly by inferior servants!"

As she finished speaking, she walked away without again looking at the Sheikh.

Nevertheless she was conscious of him behind her as she moved down the quay to where there were carriages for hire and Signor Dira was already procuring one for her.

Only as they drove away did he say apprehensively,

"That was an insult that the Sheikh will not forget!"

"What was an insult?" Vita enquired.

She felt breathless and her heart was thumping a little because the Sheikh had made her angry.

"You called one of his tribe 'an inferior servant'. That, like blood money, is punishable by a fine."

Vita laughed,

"It is unlikely the Sheikh will punish me," she said. "But it would be interesting to know what he would expect as compensation."

"For an insulting expression the usual fine is one sheep," Signor Dira replied.

Vita laughed again.

"Then the Sheikh will be disappointed, for I have no sheep. And, if I had been speaking to the groom himself, I would have been much more insulting, I assure you!"

"You must be careful, *signorina*," Signor Dira said. "In Syria memories are long and a Sheikh is very powerful."

"I assure you I am not in the least afraid of him," Vita replied, "and perhaps in future he will be more careful who he entrusts his horses to."

Signor Dira said nothing, but Vita knew that he was apprehensive.

She, however, forgot the whole episode when they visited some stables and started to bargain for the horses and the services of the men who were to escort them to Damascus.

Finally it was all arranged, and as soon as Vita and Signor Dira had eaten a meal in the nearest hotel, Vita changed into a riding habit and was ready to start.

They rode off in style and at a brisk pace.

Signor Dira had engaged a large retinue of out-riders, horses and several donkeys, which seemed unnecessary, except that Vita realised that he was nervous and determined to have as many protective elements about him as possible.

He had engaged no baggage camels, such as were usual on a caravan, since Vita had so little luggage and her valise was carried by a white donkey, which she was told denoted her to be a lady of standing.

Camels would most definitely have slowed their progress.

As soon as they climbed from the City of Beirut up into the hills, Vita was thrilled with the beauty of it all.

Never had she imagined a country could be so lovely with its high-peaked mountains covered in snow, its flowering shrubs and bushes and its trees of almond blossom pink and fairy-like against the blue of the sky.

The road was rough and there was a succession of chasms and gorges on either side of it.

It was also very warm until, as they rode higher and higher, it became quite cold and Vita was glad of the warm cloak, which Signor Dira had advised her to bring to put over her thin riding habit.

She had deliberately chosen her most spectacular habit, because she realised that the Arabs loved colour. It was a deep rose pink, frogged with white.

Her hat, very fashionable with its high crown, had a gauze veil, which encircled it and fell down at the back, protecting her a little from the rays of the sun.

Vita realised they had a long rough ride ahead and Signor Dira had already informed her that she would have to spend the night in a tent.

There were no hostelries where a lady could stay, he explained, and one of the reasons why they needed a large retinue was so that two men could be on watch all night.

To Vita it was all a wonderful adventure and, because she was used to spending long days in the saddle out hunting, it did not tire her unduly.

In the evening the sunset was superb and the colours in the sky seemed reflected in the valley they were passing through.

A large pool of clean water was encircled by sheep, cows, donkeys and camels, all drinking their fill before darkness fell.

It had been a tiring day, but Vita was in fact still full of energy and excited interest when finally they decided to camp for the night.

They had only stopped twice on the journey in order to eat.

She learnt that the usual Arab food for a caravan on the move was *djereisha*, boiled wheat that had been coarsely ground, over which melted butter was poured. If milk was added it was called *nekaa*.

She thought it would taste unpleasant but actually it was delicious and, because she was European, Signor Dira had also provided her with fruit, eggs and cheese, which he had bought in Beirut.

He explained that often travellers roasted a lamb, but he considered it a mistake to light a fire, which might draw attention to themselves.

Vita was not in the least hungry after she had eaten what was provided for her. At the same time she would have liked to see a lamb roasted and would in fact have enjoyed the warmth of the fire.

When the sun had gone down, the wind from the snow on the mountains was bitingly cold and she was glad when a small tent had been erected for her and she crept into it to find that the soft cushions that had been laid on the ground were very comfortable.

The men lay down on the ground with their heads resting against a bundle and each covered himself with his *burnouse*.

They slept with their guns close beside them and, as Vita had noticed when they left Beirut, their wide girdles each held a pistol and the curved knife called a *sekin*.

Vita was so tired that she fell asleep immediately.

*

She was woken by the sound of voices, the horses neighing and a donkey braying.

It was dawn and the whole camp was packing up ready to move on. The men were laughing and singing. Only Signor Dira looked tired, as if he had not slept well.

"You are all right, *signore*?" Vita asked him.

He smiled.

"I have grown unused to rising so early, *signorina*. Cities spoil one for the desert."

"Would you like to come back and live here?"

"Sometimes I dream of it," he replied, "but I have an Italian wife and six children who would dislike it very much!"

There seemed to be no answer to that, Vita thought, and quite soon she was back in the saddle and pushing ahead towards Damascus.

She had expected Damascus to be beautiful.

She had read that it was called 'the Pearl of the East' and that it had been written of the City, '*Oh, Damascus, though old as history itself, thou art fresh as the breath of spring*!'

It was impossible too not to feel that she had achieved something very unusual, having journeyed alone over the mountains from Beirut to reach *Shaum Sheref*, the Holy or Blessed One.

As if he knew what she was thinking, Signor Dira brought his horse alongside Vita's to say,

"The Prophet Mohammed is said to have gazed on Damascus and called it Paradise!"

"It is beautiful!" Vita exclaimed.

She was looking not only at Damascus but also at the desert around it where she thought that she could see a number of black tents in the distance.

It was still not midday when they rode into the City and Vita learnt for the first time that Cousin Jane did not live actually inside Damascus hut just outside the City gates at Bab Menzel Khassab.

She was sorry in a way that she was not to see more of the City itself, feeling that her first impressions were more exciting than they would he later, but she told herself that her first action must be to get in touch with her cousin.

She therefore allowed Signor Dira to lead her, followed by the caravan of horses and donkeys, to Bab Menzel Khassab, where Jane's house stood in extensive grounds screened from the outside world by tall trees and flowering shrubs.

As soon as she entered through the gates, Vita realised that Cousin Jane had brought a little piece of England to the desert.

There were deep herbaceous borders and beds of pinks, Sweet William, Candytuft and Canterbury bells.

There were also, Vita could see at a glance as she rode under shady trees and past lily ponds, a number of rare plants and fruit trees that must be quite alien to Syria.

Then the house came in view and it delighted her because she could see that the main portion of it was entirely Arab.

They rode up to the door and, only as they did so, did Vita realise somewhat apprehensively that the house had most of its windows shuttered and a somehow unlived-in look.

One of their retinue dismounted to peal a large iron bell.

They could hear it ringing far away in the distance and then there was a long, long wait before shuffling footsteps came to their ears over an uncarpeted floor.

Bolts were drawn back, chains released and the door opened.

An aged servant stood there and Signor Dira addressed him in Arabic.

After a long exchange of words that Vita found impossible to follow, Signor Dira turned to her apprehensively.

"I am afraid, *signorina*, you will be disappointed, but the Honourable Jane Digby El Mezrab has left for the desert.

"She is not here!" Vita cried in consternation.

She saw now how foolish it had been of her to assume that Cousin Jane would be in Damascus.

She might have anticipated that at this time of the year she would be in the desert with her Sheikh and his tribe.

Just for a moment Vita felt alarmed, fearing that her whole journey had been fruitless and that she must return to Naples.

But then with an undefeatable courage she said,

"In which case I must join my cousin. But first we must find out where she is!"

"You will join her?" Signor Dira asked in surprise.

"Of course!" Vita answered positively.

Again there was a long conversation with the servant, before finally he said,

"The man suggests that the most likely persons to know where your honourable cousin is to be found are the British Consul, Captain Richard Burton and his wife. The servant says that they are close friends and should be able to help you."

"Then we will go and find Captain and Mrs. Burton," Vita said. "Please thank the servant."

She looked rather wistfully at the house, wishing she could see inside it, but she thought it would be impertinent to suggest it.

Meekly followed by the caravan, she went back down the drive and out of the lovely grounds with their English appearance to find another house outside the City at the Kurd village of Salahiyyeh.

It was fortunately not far and, as they rode on, Vita tried to remember all she had heard about Richard Burton.

He was, like Cousin Jane, one of the people most talked about in England.

There had been articles about him in all the newspapers, and he was also a controversial personality, which made Vita know that many of the things being said about him were suppressed when she was present.

He was, she was aware, one of the world's greatest travellers, an Orientalist who wore the green turban of the *Hadj*, meaning that he had penetrated as a pilgrim the "Holy of Holies" – Mecca – and the man who had discovered the source of the Nile.

She remembered her father saying at dinner when her Cousin Bevil was staying with them,

"Did you meet Burton when you were in Syria?"

"Of course!" Bevil replied. "Who could be in Damascus without meeting him? He is fantastic! A strange disturbing man who is a legend in his own lifetime."

"You liked him?" Sir George had asked.

Bevil had shrugged his shoulders,

"Does one like a caged lion or a tiger, a man who is described as having the 'brow of a God and the jaw of a devil'?"

He had laughed, and added,

"Richard Burton is brilliant, there is no doubt about that! He speaks no less than twenty-eight languages."

"So I have heard," Sir George said dryly, "and it is always added in the Club that one of them is pornography."

Having forgotten, as he spoke, that Vita was present, he coughed and changed the subject.

Vita felt excited that besides meeting Cousin Jane she would meet this man as well, who had caused such a sensation, but whose books she was forbidden to read under any circumstances whatsoever.

She did not know why they were banned, except that there were whispers about Richard Burton's behaviour, as there were about her cousin's.

She had heard someone say that he had actually entered a harem in disguise, besides taking part in strange native rituals that no white man had ever seen and remained alive.

The Kurd village was very beautiful and, as Vita rode through the narrow streets, where they were obliged to travel single file, she saw a small Mosque and adjoining it the house she sought.

There were cascades of roses and vines adorning the walls and, as they rode into the arcaded courtyard, there was a fountain playing, its water iridescent in the sun.

Once again a bell was pulled which echoed away in a building by no means as impressive or as large as Cousin Jane's had been, but undoubtedly attractive.

Looking round, Vita saw a strange assortment of animals.

There were lambs moving about in the garden, small and thin, as if they had been brought in because they were too weak to fend for themselves in a flock.

There were baby goats, a deer that seemed quite unafraid amongst the other animals, a large number of dogs and several fat cats asleep on the windowsills.

It was later that Vita was to learn that there was also a leopard amongst the pets!

A servant opened the door and Signor Dira explained why Vita had journeyed to Damascus. The man seemed to expect them to enter and Vita dismounted from the saddle.

She stepped into the cool arched hall and a moment later a large, plump, middle-aged woman came forward, both hands outstretched.

"Did I hear your Courier say that you are a cousin of Jane Digby El Mezrab?" she asked.

"Yes I am," Vita answered. "I have come to Syria especially to see her only to find that she is not at home but has left for the desert. I want to join her and I hope that you will be able to help me."

"'But, of course, I will help you. I am Isobel Burton. Any relative of dear Jane's is a friend of mine! But you are beautiful and very like your cousin."

Isobel Burton was not only large, she was also over powering.

She swept Vita into the sitting room, sent for refreshments, asked her a hundred questions without waiting for an answer and chatted away with a friendliness that was quite disarming. It also mitigated the fact that she was undeniably, insatiably curious.

"I was in Naples and so I thought it would be nice to meet my relative, of whom I have heard so much," Vita said demurely.

She had no intention of saying too much to this voluble woman. At the same time she was well aware that, if she was to find Jane, it was Isobel Burton who could help her to do so.

"Jane has been gone for nearly three weeks," Mrs. Burton was explaining. "We had a delightful summer before she left! We sat on the roof under the stars, talking until very late."

"I should be very grateful if you would help me to find Cousin Jane as soon as possible?" Vita said. "Do you think she is far away?"

Isobel Burton made an expressive gesture with her hands.

"It is always difficult to know where the Mezrabs will travel to at this time of the year, but I do not think they will be far. The pasture land is good quite near the City and they will exhaust that first before they move further on."

"I am anxious to leave quickly," Vita said. "If possible today."

Mrs. Burton shook her head.

"It is too late in the day to set out now," she replied, "and besides, I doubt if the men who brought you from Beirut will consent to go further."

"You mean I shall have to engage others?"

"Yes," Mrs. Burton replied, "but there will be no difficulty about that."

She looked at Vita and smiled.

"You are very young and very lovely," she said. "Most people would be horrified at the idea of your going off alone into the desert."

"Why?" Vita asked.

"They would try to frighten you with tales of travellers being harried, plundered and even killed."

"Are such stories true?" Vita asked.

Isobel Burton laughed.

"Your Cousin Jane will tell you the truth about the desert and I love the Bedouins as she does."

"Then you will help me find her?"

"I will get in touch with one of Sheikh Medjuel's men, who will arrange a caravan for you. It will be expensive, I am afraid."

Mrs. Burton waited a little anxiously until Vita replied,

"That is not important!"

"Leave it all to me," Mrs. Burton smiled. "I am used to arranging things. My husband relies on me completely and I promise you that will be well looked after.|"

"Then I would like to leave tomorrow morning as early as possible," Vita said, "if you are sure it would not be too much trouble for you to keep me here tonight."

"It will be a pleasure!" Mrs. Burton replied. "You must tell me all about England! Oh dear, how much I miss the Social scene, the parties, the balls and the Court gossip!"

It was quite obvious to Vita by the end of the evening that Isobel Burton was a snob.

She was determined to make it very clear how close a friend she was of Jane and Vita had the feeling that to Mrs. Burton Cousin Jane would always be 'Lady Ellenborough, a Peeress', rather than 'the wife of a Mezrab'.

At the same time Mrs. Burton told her fascinating stories about her cousin.

She related how Jane hunted with her Sheikh and her Persian hounds, shot partridges, raced dromedaries – a very difficult feat – could speak Arabic perfectly and rode at the head of the tribe into war.

"She can also milk camels," Mrs. Burton finished, while Vita gasped in astonishment.

"What a number of pets you have!" Vita remarked later and learnt of another side of Cousin Jane's character.

"Not as many as Jane," Mrs. Burton replied. "Besides horses, donkeys, dromedaries, Persian hounds, parrots and a tame pelican, who is famous in Damascus, there are a hundred cats!"

"A hundred!" Vita exclaimed.

"Each one has his own plate!" Mrs. Burton completed.

"Tell me what Cousin Jane looks like," Vita begged.

"She is beautiful, commanding and Queen-like," Mrs. Burton answered. "The Bedouins called her *Umn-el-Lalan* – mother of milk – because of her white skin. Your skin is white too. Jane must have looked exactly like you at your age."

Vita did not want to talk about herself and it was with a feeling of intense curiosity that she turned to Richard Burton.

He was in fact the most remarkable man she had ever met.

He had very dark hair, black, clearly-defined eyebrows and a brown, weather-beaten complexion. There were deep hollows beneath his cheekbones and he had an enormous black moustache.

Perhaps his most remarkable features, she thought, were his two large, black, staring eyes with long black eyelashes, which seemed, when he looked at her, to pierce her through and through.

She found herself remembering another pair of eyes she had looked into yesterday. Those of Sheikh Shaa-lan El Hassein and she recalled the expression of contempt on his face as he looked her up and down.

It was certainly a look of hostility and she wondered why she, of all people, should evoke such a look from a man, especially an Arab, who she had always believed admired fair women.

She longed to ask Richard Burton what he thought of him, but instead she related how badly the horse had been looked after on the voyage and how the Sheikh had been surprised when she told him.

"The Sheikhs are usually extra careful about their stallions," he said, "especially those that are pure-bred. But Sheikh Shaa-lan is a strange man. He is an avowed enemy of Medjuel El Mezrab, so I should say little about him when you join your cousin."

"You are giving Miss Ashford entirely the wrong idea," Mrs. Burton interposed. "Medjuel, like dear Jane, is the kindest person possible. He hates feuds."

"I hardly think Sheikh Shaa-lan would agree with that!" Richard Burton said with a note of impatience in his voice.

Vita thought that he found his wife's interpretation of the Arab mind irritating.

Mrs. Burton was very eager, when they were alone, to talk intimately of Sheikh Medjuel.

"He is charming, educated and a very intelligent man – but as a husband – !"

"You mean because he is an Arab?"

"Yes, dear, that dark skin – But Jane literally worships him, so of course she is very jealous."

"Has she reason to be?" Vita asked.

She remembered that Bedouins could have four wives and could divorce them with one sentence.

"No, I don't think so." Isobel Burton, however, sounded doubtful. "But poor dear Jane is fanatically suspicious of Ouadijid. She is the very attractive widow of Medjuel's son Schebibb."

She paused to add,

"When one is passionately and romantically in love, it is difficult not to be jealous."

There was a throb in her voice that told Vita she was thinking of herself.

Then she said, as if the thought had just struck her,

"Of course Jane may find it difficult not to be jealous of you. It is not always pleasant when one is over sixty to see oneself recreated at eighteen."

Vita stared at Mrs. Burton wide-eyed as such an idea had never entered her mind.

Then she dismissed it as absurd!

She was, however, too excited about what was to happen tomorrow to wish to sit up late, even to talk about Cousin Jane.

So having with difficulty freed herself of Isobel Burton, she crept into bed and fell asleep almost immediately.

*

She was woken soon after dawn to find the house buzzing with activity and that Richard Burton, surprisingly, had already left for Damascus.

Mrs. Burton was busy feeding her animals.

"They are my children, my beloved children," she said with a whimsical smile.

After a quick breakfast, Vita found a large caravan waiting outside the house to escort her into the desert.

She gathered from the bill that was presented to her that there had been an enormous amount of things to buy that were necessary to their journey.

Signor Dira was there to see her off.,

"You are quite certain you will not change your mind and come with me, *signore*?" Vita asked with a smile.

"I wish it was possible," he replied, "but I have my family in Naples and I also have a chance of joining a caravan that is leaving for Damascus this morning. It will be safer for me to travel with them."

Knowing how fearful he was, Vita did not try to persuade him any further but merely thanked him for his kindness and for the Arabic that he had taught her.

"You are the best pupil I have ever had, *signorina*," he said. "The man who goes with you will continue your lessons. I have already spoken to him about it."

The man in question, who was apparently in charge of the caravan, looked older than Signor Dira, but had more authority about him, Vita thought.

However, Mrs. Burton, when she came to inspect Vita's retinue, was clearly not impressed.

"You are not the man I engaged yesterday," she said sharply, "Where is Yousef?"

"Yousef is ill, Excellency," the man replied. "He sends his deepest apologies, but is not well enough to undertake the journey."

"That is absurd, as you well know!" Isobel Burton said sharply. "Either he has had an offer of more money or he has personal reasons for not joining the tribe."

"I am Nasir, Excellency, I will escort the lady. There is no difficulty. I know the desert like the back of my hand."

"I only hope you are right," Mrs. Burton said in an ominous tone.

Then turning to Vita, she said in a low voice,

"This is extremely irritating. I saw Yousef last night and he promised to arrange everything himself and to accompany you."

Vita looked at the collection of horses, all of which seemed to her to be fine specimens. The elderly Bedouin also looked reliable.

"I am sure it will be all right," she said soothingly.

"I don't like my plans being altered," Mrs. Burton said. "Yousef promised me that he would go with you. There is absolutely no excuse for him to have changed his mind in under twelve hours."

"Perhaps he really is ill," Vita suggested.

"Nonsense!" Isobel Burton said. "He just has some reason for not wishing to leave Damascus and I assure you I will find out what it is!"

Vita was quite certain that the threat would be put into practice, but, as she did not wish to wait any longer, she said goodbye to her hostess and thanked her profusely.

Then, mounting the horse that was waiting for her, she realised with a sense of delight that it was a particularly fine Arabian thoroughbred.

'I am sure it is because I am going to Cousin Jane that I have such a splendid animal,' she thought to herself. 'I don't believe it is Mrs. Burton's orders that matter so much as Sheikh Medjuel's!'

They rode away, Vita waving as she went.

Soon they were free of the small village and out into the open desert.

There was something inexplicably thrilling about seeing the sand in front of her undulating away into the barren mountains on one side and into an indefinable horizon in front.

Behind the spires and domes of Damascus were translucent as pearls in the rays of the rising sun.

Chapter Four

The caravan set off at a sharp pace and Vita found it thrilling to be riding such a fine animal. She felt full of vitality in the cool air of the dawn.

The sun was rising, but it was not yet hot. They galloped over the soft ground, moving gradually away from the pasture land that surrounded Damascus out into the desert itself.

'It is exactly as thought it would be!' Vita thought. 'And even more romantic!'

There were strange colours that she had not expected, which gave the horizon a mystical translucency that she could not identify with anything that she had ever seen before.

She had expected the desert to be flat, but it was in fact undulating with occasional sharp rocks rising out of nowhere, sometimes surrounded by rough patches of scrubland.

Then again unexpectedly there was green pasture where sheep were grazing and where in the distance Vita could see clusters of tents.

She thought that they must be part of the Aeneze tribe, but Nasir had apparently no intention of wasting time by conversing with the Bedouins they met on the way and chose a route that gave Vita no chance of seeing them closer.

At first it was difficult to converse with the middle-aged man who was escorting her because the horses were moving so swiftly.

She was to learn that Arabian horses always wished to gallop and that trotting or cantering was something they did not understand.

The other men who had been engaged seemed to keep themselves apart as if they were embarrassed at being in her presence.

As they rode on, she saw some of the desert animals and Nasir explained their names in Arabic.

There were ostriches, usually too far away for Vita to see them clearly, but Nasir told her that the male had black feathers with white tips, except for the tail feathers, which were wholly white.

"And the females?" Vita asked.

"Her feathers are spotted grey," he replied.

Nasir went on to tell her that the female bred in the middle of winter and laid from twelve to twenty-one eggs.

"The Bedouins reckon them as delicious food and they are sold for about one shilling each."

"And the feathers? Are the feathers valuable?" Vita enquired.

"The finest are sold singly," Nasir replied, "and fetch from one to two shillings in the market."

Besides the ostriches Vita saw quite a number of gazelles.

There were also two or three wild asses, but they did not appear to her to be very different from the ordinary domestic animal.

There were plenty of storks, wild geese, partridges and larks and there were hundreds of birds, which Nasir told her were called *kattahs*. They appeared like a cloud in the distance and, she learnt, laid their eggs in stony districts.

"The eggs are very popular," Nasir explained. "Arabs eat great quantities of them."

When the horses allowed them to talk, Vita asked questions about the plants, trying to remember their names, like *shaumar* which was something like fennel, and *wasbe* which had a yellow stalk. Nasir told her it stained the camels' mouths black when they ate it.

But after a time conversation was too difficult and Vita contented herself with thinking what she would say to Cousin Jane when she found her.

She could not help remembering a little uncomfortably that Isobel Burton had thought that her cousin would be jealous of her.

Thinking it over, Vita was certain that it was an absurd idea. After all, no one had lived a fuller, more exciting or dramatic life than Jane Digby.

Nothing could be more satisfying, Vita thought, than to own such a beautiful house in Damascus and at the same time to be the *Sitt* or Queen of her husband's tribe so that she could accompany him out into the desert.

How could Vita at eighteen possibly compete with anyone so important or indeed so beautiful?

People had said to Vita that she resembled Jane, but, although she received a number of compliments, she was not acknowledged a world beauty as Jane had been nor had she queues of admirers seeking to marry her or to place a Royal Crown at her feet.

'I have only Lord Bantham,' Vita thought and felt that he was a poor substitute for all the famous, distinguished and exciting men who had loved her cousin.

Equally she was very young and, although Charles might think Cousin Jane was too old for love, it was obvious from what both Bevil and Mrs. Burton had said that at sixty-two she was still romantic, passionate and perhaps possessive.

The idea that Jane might look on her as a rival left an uncomfortable feeling in Vita's mind and she continued to ruminate about it until at midday they stopped at a small oasis.

The water was drawn for the horses by lowering a bucket on a long rope down into the depths of a well and pulling it full to the surface.

For Vita drinking water was carried in a strangely-shaped goatskin bottle. It tasted rather unpleasant, so she drank as little as possible.

The same sort of food that she had eaten the previous day was prepared for her and they rested under the shade of the palms from the intense heat of the day.

After they resumed their journey in about two hours, Vita saw on the horizon first a cloud of dust and then a number of men riding towards them on horseback.

She turned to speak to Nasir and ask him if he knew who was approaching, when to her surprise she found that he was not beside her but apparently had moved to the very back of the horsemen following.

She called him, but apparently he did not hear, for he did not come forward, while the other riders seemed to close around her.

"Where is Nasir?" she asked impatiently, then realising that they did not understand, she repeated his name several times.

Again she was not answered and she thought that the men riding beside her were not interested in what she had to say, but were watching the horsemen who were approaching them.

They came a little nearer and suddenly Vita remembered all that Bevil had told her about the tribes who attacked travellers, dividing so that the first half stole their possessions, while the other half pretended to rescue them and so be rewarded for doing so.

She wondered if this was what the horsemen ahead of them intended and once again she called for Nasir.

She turned round on her saddle as she did so, determined to see what was preventing him from coming to her side.

Then to her utter astonishment she saw him riding away, back the way they had come as fast as his horse could carry him.

She was so astounded that for a moment she could only stare.

Then the sound of pistol shots made her turn again to where now she could see the men galloping violently towards them at full speed.

They were firing as they did so, yelling, hanging over their stirrups with their bridles in their teeth, waving their long feathered lances in the air, throwing them and catching them again at full gallop!

Vita was terrified.

Her horse was fidgety, excited by the noise, and, as she attempted to control him, she remembered hearing when people were talking of Cousin Jane, of the *djerid* or *fantasia*

– the wild plunging charge of the Bedouin horsemen, which was practised from Morocco to Arabia.

Now some of the riders were throwing themselves under their horses' bellies, firing at full gallop, yelling and shouting what must obviously be a war cry.

Without being really conscious that she did so, Vita had forced her horse to a standstill and the men who were with her did the same.

Just as Vita felt that the Bedouins must ride right into them in what would be a disastrous and unavoidable collision, they pulled their mounts back on their haunches.

It was a brilliant display of horsemanship, but extremely unnerving and Vita realised that her whole body was tense.

One close look at the horsemen, however, told her that there was little to fear. They were young men, handsome with their flashing dark eyes and smiling lips that revealed glistening white teeth.

They may have appeared ferocious in the distance, but now she saw that they were obviously friendly.

What was more, the men who escorted her were making no effort to fight the newcomers. In fact not one of them had drawn the pistols that they carried in their girdles.

Vita waited because there was nothing else she could do.

At the same time she wondered frantically what was the explanation.

Then one horseman, who appeared to be in charge, gave a word of command and the rest encircled Vita and her escort while he rode ahead.

He made it clear that they were intended to follow him and Vita told herself the explanation was obvious.

These men must have be sent by Sheikh Medjuel to bring her into camp.

That he should have learnt in advance of her arrival was, she was certain, something that frequently happened in the desert.

Perhaps someone had reached his camping place from Damascus to say that she was on the way. Perhaps they had a method of communication of their own, like a special courier pigeon service, which had been in use for generations after being established by the Fatimid Caliphs of Cairo.

Bevil had told her that the birds flew in relays, Cairo – Basra – Beirut – Constantinople, and on the desert routes from Damascus to Palmyra there were bird-towers every fifty miles.

Whoever they might be, it was obvious to Vita that these were not enemies but friends.

Immediately she was interested in their horses and in the colourful appearance of the men who rode them.

The only thing she could not understand was why Nasir had run away.

He had not seemed the sort of man who would be fearful and, as he was a Mezrab, surely he should have recognised his own tribe the moment they were sighted in the distance?

She could not understand, but her Arabic was not good enough for her to ask questions and she told herself confidently that there would be plenty of time for it all to be explained to her when she reached the Sheikh's camp.

She was surprised, however, that they were travelling such a long way.

Isobel Burton had been sure that Sheikh Medjuel would be not very far from Damascus where the pasturage was good and, as he and Cousin Jane had not been in the desert for more than three weeks, it seemed surprising that they should have moved so far in such a short time.

But Vita had no idea of the extent of their flocks or indeed how much pasturage would be required.

She also was not certain how numerous the tribe would be at this time of the year.

Vita knew that the Aeneze were the most powerful people in the vicinity of Syria and one of the largest bodies of Bedouins in the Arabian desert.

They were, however, divided into many different tribes of which the Mezrab were only one.

Bevil had told her that the Aeneze, when he was in Syria, were estimated at three hundred souls, spread over a territory of at least forty thousand square miles.

But he did not know how large the Mezrab tribe was and Vita could only speculate about them.

They rode on and on and Vita was beginning to grow a little tired when finally she saw ahead of her something that looked like a great patch of black.

As they drew nearer, she saw that it was in fact a huge number of black tents.

They had obviously reached their destination because the horsemen quickened their pace and once again began to utter their war cries, waving their lances, throwing them in the air and catching them again.

Many of them began to sing a somewhat tuneless song, which made the others laugh.

The horses too seemed to realise that they were reaching home and soon they were galloping at full speed over the level ground that lay between them and the tents.

'I have won! I have done what I came out to do!' Vita told herself elatedly. 'Now I shall see Cousin Jane! I shall find a solution to my problems, even as she found a solution to hers!'

It seemed to her as she looked ahead that there was an enormous number of tents and she thought in fact there must be at least two or three hundred of them.

Now at last they were near enough to see one large and impressive tent facing West, a little way from the others and this Vita knew was the tent of the Sheikh.

Signor Dira had told her that the Chief's or Sheikh's tent was always on the Western side of the camp, for it was from the West, he explained, that the Syrian Arabs expected their enemies as well as their guests.

"To fight the former and to honour the latter is the Sheikh's principal business," he said. "It is considered disgraceful that a brave leader should pitch his tent on the Eastern side of his camp."

Vita had not thought the information particularly interesting at the time, but now she was glad to see the large tent and to know that she had to ride no further.

It had been a long day and, as the horsemen, still uttering their war cries, drew up in front of the tent, she dismounted and, giving a quick touch to her hat to see that it was in place, she was ready to enter.

There were Bedouins who were obviously servants standing on either side of the open flap to lei her pass.

Then, as she walked in eagerly, it was to find one man standing in the centre of the tent waiting for her.

She had one quick glance at him and her heart gave a frightened leap, for it was not Cousin Jane who stood there, nor was it Sheikh Abdul Medjuel El Mezrab.

Instead it was Sheikh Shaa-lan El Hassein, whom she had last spoken to on the quay at Beirut.

For a moment they stood looking at each other.

Then without thinking, because she was so astonished, Vita spoke in English.

"Why am I here?" she asked.

"You are my prisoner!" the Sheikh replied in the same language.

"Y-your – prisoner? "

Vita found it hard to say the words and, as she stared at him incredulously, she saw the same look of contempt and hostility on his face that she had noticed when she spoke to him on the quayside.

"You speak English!" she said.

It was the first thought that had come into her mind.

"We can revert to conversing in French, if you prefer," he replied.

Vita drew in a deep breath.

"Why – why have you – brought me here, and how dare you prevent me from reaching my cousin, as I wish to do!"

"Your cousin is married to Abdul Medjuel El Mezrab, who is my enemy," the Sheikh replied. "Shall we say it is more satisfactory to steal an honoured guest and a relation by marriage than to take his sheep or his horses?"

It was the way he spoke more than what he said that made Vita angry.

"How dare you make me a part of your pettifogging tribal warfare!" she exclaimed. "I am in Syria to see my cousin and I request you, because I am a British Subject, to take me to her immediately!"

She spoke with what she thought was a note of authority and after a moment the Sheikh replied,

"Of course, the fact that you are a British Subject should be more effective than an Army of soldiers. It may be in some parts of the world, but not here!"

"You have absolutely no right to kidnap me – in this outrageous manner!" Vita said angrily.

"It was not very difficult," the Sheikh remarked.

There was something in the way he spoke that made Vita retort quickly,

"You planned this! Nasir is in your pay! It was you who prevented Yousef the Mezrab from taking me to his tribe as Mrs. Burton had arranged!"

She knew now why Nasir, who she had paid to guard her, had ridden off when the horsemen approached them.

They must all have been Sheikh Shaa-lan's men and not Mezrabs as she had thought.

It was a disgraceful plot, she told herself, and what was more important than anything else, it might delay her return to Naples. In which case there would be trouble with Lady Crowen and perhaps her father would be informed.

With an effort she forced herself to say,

"Could we not talk about this – sensibly?"

"It depends what you mean by 'sensibly'," the Sheikh replied. "But I am not behaving as I should to a guest. Will you not sit down? And I expect you would like a cup of coffee?"

Vita's throat was extremely dry after riding so far without a drink and, as the Sheikh made a gesture with his hand, she sat down on a *roffe*, which was like a large comfortable divan.

There was a low coffee table of beaten brass in front of it and, as she seated herself, Vita saw that a very fine Persian rug covered the floor.

The tent was larger than she had imagined it would be and it was divided by what appeared to be a hanging carpet of heavy white wool interwoven with patterns of flowers.

Because she was feeling tired and at the same time realising that she must have all her wits about her, she took off her high-crowned riding hat and set it down at her side.

She had arranged her hair very carefully when she had dressed in the morning so that despite a long day's riding it was not untidy or falling at the back in wisps, as many women's did after a hard day's hunting.

She was also aware that her pink riding habit still looked fresh and uncreased despite the long hours she had been in the saddle, and yet she knew that for some unaccountable reason her appearance did not arouse any admiration in the man facing her.

He had also seated himself and now a black slave came in carrying the coffee.

Vita knew that all the Arab Sheikhs of importance employed slaves, but she had never seen one before and she looked at the woman with interest as she poured out the coffee, then bowed low to the Sheikh and left the tent.

The coffee was hot and delicious and they sat in silence until Vita had drunk half a cupful.

Then she said,

"How much money – do you require to set me free?"

"I thought perhaps you intended to offer me money," the Sheikh said. "I doubt, even if you are as rich as your cousin, you would be able to bribe me."

There was something harsh and unbending in the way he spoke which made Vita feel that she was up against someone so inflexible that it would be impossible for her to make any impression on him.

But desperately she had to try.

"Then what can I – offer you?" she asked.

"Nothing!" he replied. "You will write to your cousin, telling her of your plight and informing her that you are the prisoner of El Hassein. After that we wait until her husband and his followers come to rescue you."

"You intend to use me to start a war?" Vita enquired.

"That is my intention," the Sheikh replied.

"How can you be so childish – so ridiculous – as to want to cause bloodshed for no reason whatsoever?"

Vita looked out through the open flap of the tent to where the desert undulated away towards Damascus, from where she had come.

"This is the time of year when the tribes are feeding their flocks," she went on. "Why can you not let them – do so in peace? Men like you are bloodthirsty! It is cruel and senseless to want to fight for no better reason than that you have been enemies for centuries."

"You are very eloquent," the Sheikh remarked and she knew that he was sneering at her.

He spoke English with an accent, but he was, she realised, extremely fluent.

And yet it made what he said seem even more forceful than if he had spoken in French, which was a softer and more flowery language.

It was obvious, Vita thought, that defiance was going to get her nowhere.

Instead she tried another tack.

"I am going to appeal to you," she said softly, "to let me go to my cousin or, if you like, return to Damascus. If I do not do so quickly, I shall be in very grave trouble. However much you may dislike the Mezrab, there is no reason why I should suffer as the scapegoat – for their crimes."

"What sort of trouble?" the Sheikh asked.

For a moment Vita hesitated and then she told him the truth.

"I have run away from my chaperone and the Courier chosen for me by my father. I left them in Naples and came here to see my cousin because I have certain personal problems that I wish to discuss with her. Send me to her camp – please send me – and afterwards, when I am gone, you can carry on with your war, if you wish to do so."

"You are most persuasive," the Sheikh said, "but if you held a trump card in your hand as I do, would you discard it so readily? And indeed so senselessly!"

"It is not senseless to me," Vita said, "and I have offered you money."

"In which I have no interest," he answered, "although I daresay it would buy me a few more guns to shoot down your cousin's tribe with!"

He was being deliberately provocative, Vita thought, but with an effort she did not answer him rudely.

Instead she rose to her feet to walk across the tent and stand at the opening.

The sun was sinking and the sable of the night was already creeping up the sky.

There was no twilight in the desert. One moment it was light and the next moment it would be dark.

"Are you thinking of running away?" she heard the Sheikh ask behind her.

"Why not?" she asked. "It would be better than to stay here to be made a cat's paw."

"You would not get far."

There was something in the way he said it that made her turn round to look up at him, half apprehensively, half angrily.

"Are you threatening me with physical violence?" she asked.

"Why not?" he answered.

"Because it is an outrage! I have already told you I am a British subject. You may think you are immune from law and order, but I promise you that, if you keep me prisoner, it will cause so much trouble – that you will regret it to your dying day!"

"That is really a challenge!" the Sheikh sneered.

He put out his hands and Vita knew that he was going to take hold of her.

She gave a scream of sheer fury.

Then she was not quite certain how it happened, but she was fighting, struggling with him, attempting to tear herself free of him, but conscious all the time of his superior strength.

After her first cry, she did not scream again and they were both silent, wrestling together as Vita strove to free herself from his arms and from his robes which seemed to envelop her, so that it was hard to breathe.

She beat with her fists against his chest and yet at the same time she was conscious that she was as ineffectual as a bird beating its wings against the bars of a cage.

Slowly, relentlessly, he pulled her back into the tent, across it and then when she least expected it, tumbled her backwards onto the *roffe* and threw himself on top of her.

Still she went on fighting until, with a feeling of hopelessness, she realised that her strength was going and she was too breathless and exhausted to fight any more.

Then, with a sudden burst of energy, she struggled frantically to thrust him from her. Only to be aware that the weight of his body brought her a feeling of utter helplessness and she knew that everything was going black and that she was losing consciousness.

It was then that she heard him say grimly as if the words were forced from between his teeth,

"And now, Elaine, will you deny that I am your Master?"

The words seemed far away and suddenly Vita could fight no more.

She felt herself giving in, felt the darkness flooding over her.

Yet a sudden terror of what might happen now that she had surrendered made her gasp piteously,

"Please – *please* – !"

Even as she spoke, her eyes closed and she was still.

The Sheikh looked down at her pale exhausted face and rose, leaving her spread-eagled on the *roffè*.

"You are safe enough from me if that is what you fear," he said in a hard, bitter voice. "As a virgin you are more valuable as a hostage and men fight better for a woman who is pure."

Dimly in the darkness which seemed to be encompassing her, Vita heard what he said.

Then a second later he added,

"Anyway, I can assure you I am not interested in fair-haired, blue-eyed women. I leave them to Medjuel El Mezrab!"

As he spoke, he went from the tent, leaving her alone.

*

It was some minutes before Vita could move, before the darkness which had hovered over her seemed to disperse a little and she raised herself from the *roffè*.

She felt as if every muscle was aching intolerably from her struggle with the Sheikh.

She knew that there would be bruises on her arms the next day and, as she pulled herself to a sitting position, she thought that her body would be bruised too.

She had never imagined it possible that she would fight with a man in such a manner and she could not understand how they had become so entangled or why the argument between them had ceased being one of words and become instead one of action.

Her head was swimming and once again she shut her eyes to steady herself.

When she opened them, she saw that a Bedouin woman had come into the tent.

She was wearing a blue shapeless garment and she had dark hair in long plaits on either side or her face, hanging almost to the ground.

She bowed to Vita and made a gesture, which she understood as inviting her to move somewhere else.

The woman pulled aside the white woollen curtain and Vita found herself in another part of the tent in what she felt must be the guest room.

There was a cushioned divan with a silk cover and there was a low table beside it and washing appliances in one corner.

Besides these Vita saw that her valise had been placed on the floor.

When she opened it, looking for soap and sponges to wash with, she was so tired that she was glad that the Bedouin woman was there to help her out of her riding habit.

One of the sleeves was torn at the shoulder where she had struggled with the Sheikh and the woman explained in sign language that she would mend it.

Vita was so exhausted that, after she had washed, she would have liked to lie down on the bed, but it was obvious from the signs the woman made to her that she was expected to put on another gown and she supposed that this would entail dinner with the Sheikh.

When she thought about it, she decided that she was hungry.

But, because she was still so weak, she thought it would help if she had another cup of coffee.

Coffee was fortunately a word she knew in Arabic, having learnt it from Signor Dira and, smiling, the woman hurried to fetch it.

It certainly dissipated some of Vita's fatigue, but her arms still hurt from her fight with the Sheikh.

When she looked at herself in the mirror she carried in her valise she saw that she was very pale and had dark lines under her eyes.

It was, however, she told herself, of little consequence what she looked like.

She knew only too well what the Sheikh thought of her.

At the same time she could not help wondering who Elaine was.

She supposed that the Sheikh had uttered her name inadvertently and that perhaps one of the reasons he had fought so violently with her was that in his mind he was fighting Elaine, whoever she might be.

'Perhaps I am being over-imaginative,' Vita told herself.

It was, however, difficult to think clearly, and, when finally she was dressed, in a pretty gown she had brought with her hoping that Cousin Jane would admire it, she wondered whether she would not be wiser to refuse to meet the Sheikh again and retire instead to bed.

She had an uncomfortable feeling that, if he wished to see her, it would not stop him whether she was in bed or not. It would be best therefore to do what he wished.

Her dress was a pale pink and swept back in the new fashion, which gave it a slight bustle.

It was not an evening gown, but the neck was cut in a square and it had small sleeves. The bodice fitted very tightly, revealing her slim and exquisitely curved figure.

She knew that the Bedouin woman was regarding her with admiration, which was a little consolation as she steeled herself to pass through the white woollen carpet that divided her from the Sheikh's tent.

He was waiting for her as she had expected he would be and she had another moment of panic, of desire to run away and to disappear into the desert.

But a pride that had always been part of Vita's make-up forced her to hold her head high and face him defiantly.

He looked her over and she thought that once again his eyes were hostile.

Because he did not speak and Vita felt nervous, she asked lightly,

"I hope it is time for dinner. It is a long time since I ate at an oasis on the way here."

"Dinner is ready," the Sheikh said. "But, of course, as you are in a Bedouin camp you must behave as a Bedouin woman."

She looked at him apprehensively and he said,

"You will wash my hands and feet as is the custom!"

Vita was very still.

She knew that he intended to insult her and she was well aware that a Bedouin woman would not only wash the hands and feet of her husband or Master but also wait on him.

Signor Dira had told her that a Bedouin woman never ate the best part of any dish that was provided for the men. When the men had been served, the women ate what was left in the *Meharrem*.

They never had the good fortune to taste any meat except the head, feet and liver of the lambs.

"When a stranger is entertained," the Signor had said, 'the men of the tribe participate in the supper, but the women have to beg a foot or some trifling portion of the animal killed for the occasion."

Wildly Vita wondered what she should do.

If she defied the Sheikh, she might incur again the violence she had already been subjected to.

Suddenly she thought that it would be more dignified and perhaps more disconcerting to him if she did as he asked.

"Of course!" she said forcing a faint smile to her lips. "But I am afraid that you will have to instruct me as to how to do it properly. It is not a custom that women in England find commendable!"

The Sheikh snapped his fingers and the black slave, who had attended on them when Vita had first arrived, brought in a basin and a towel.

He gave a word of command in Arabic and the slave, with a faint air of surprise, handed the bowl to Vita.

She held it out to the Sheikh and he put his fingers into the water. Then placing the bowl on the ground she dried them on a towel, which she noticed was of fine linen.

She did not look at him as she did so and, when she had finished drying his hands, she went down on her knees in front of him and placed the bowl ready at his feet.

They were bare and she realised that he had been walking in the tent without slippers, but his feet were clean and were, she thought, particularly fine-boned and narrow.

She wiped them and, looking up at him for the first time, she said,

"I am just wondering how many foot-washings equal one sheep!"

The Sheikh did not reply and she went on,

"I am well aware that I am paying for the insult. I am just considering how expensive it will prove."

There was a smile at the corner of the Sheikh's lips as he answered,

"You are free of debt!"

Vita rose to her feet.

"I am glad about that. And am I allowed to be a guest or a prisoner?"

"Do you know the difference?" the Sheikh enquired.

"Of course," Vita replied, "as a guest I will eat with you. As a prisoner I will have to wait until you are finished and I am very hungry!"

The Sheikh laughed and Vita felt that she had scored a point.

She had broken through his defences, at least for the moment, and she wondered what his next move would be.

Dinner was brought to them as they sat side by side on the *roffe*.

Fortunately Vita had learnt from Bevil how the Bedouins ate and was not dismayed when there were no knives, forks or spoons.

Lamb was the main dish, which she knew had been cooked in *burgoul* and camel's milk.

Burgoul was wheat boiled with butter or oil and dried in the sun. The wheat then was preserved for a year.

The *burgoul* was placed in a large wooden dish with thin slices of the lamb round the outside.

Vita did not find it difficult to shape the lamb into small balls with the *burgoul* and put them into her mouth.

The food was very hot and it needed care not to burn her fingers.

Because she was hungry, she thought that lamb had never tasted better.

She also enjoyed the freshly baked bread called *jisre* and several other dishes, which appeared to be made of strange ingredients that she had never eaten before.

To finish the meal there was *heneyne*, a delicious sweetmeat made of bread, butter and dates blended together.

The only drink was *leben* or sour milk.

Vita had heard of it and expected it to be unpleasant, but actually after drinking half a glass she found it not unpalatable.

Signor Dira had told her that the Bedouins considered it a stimulant, as they looked on the use of all fermented liquors as disgraceful. Coffee was, however, served immediately after the meal.

They were waited on by two slaves and Vita was glad that one of them brought her a basin to wash in when they had finished eating.

The Sheikh talked very little while the dinner was being served and the slaves were hovering around them, bringing a fresh dish every time Vita thought that the meal was at an end.

Finally, when she realised that she could eat no more, she drank her coffee and looked at the Sheikh with a smile.

"I was very hungry," she said almost as if she was excusing her own greed.

"You must be stronger than you look!" he said. "You had a long ride. Most men would have found it very tiring."

"I am indeed tired," she admitted, "but not only from riding!"

She blushed as she spoke and she then wished that she had not spoken, knowing he would understand that it was her struggle with him that had fatigued her more than anything else.

"Before you go to bed," he said, "I want you to write that letter. As you will obviously not wish to stay here longer than is necessary, the sooner it goes to Sheikh Medjuel the better!"

"Must you really – send it?" Vita asked in a low voice.

"Are you afraid that perhaps he will not think you worthy of rescue?" the Sheikh asked.

"No. I am not afraid of that," Vita answered, "I was just thinking that the war will mean not only that your men will be wounded or killed – but also your horses."

"You are still worrying in case I don't take good care of my horses?" the Sheikh asked.

"I admire them so much," Vita said. "The horses that carried us here, and those of your horsemen who tried to frighten me with a *djerid* would fetch a fortune in Tattersalls sale rooms in London. Must they be hurt by an unnecessary war?"

"War is life to a Bedouin," the Sheikh replied. "If we do not fight, my tribe will grow fat and lazy and they will lose face,"

"I should have thought that they could have found better ways to occupy themselves," Vita said sharply.

"For them it is a way of life,"

"Even though you know better?"

There was a moment's silence.

Then he said,

"Why should you say that? Why should you think I am any different from my men?"

"Because you are educated as they are not, and because you are too intelligent to say it is Fate – *Insha'Allah*. God has willed it so!"

She thought there was an expression of surprise in the Sheikh's eyes.

For a moment he looked at her and she thought that the hostility had gone.

Then he said abruptly,

"There is no other course open to you except to write as I have requested."

He snapped his fingers and a slave who had obviously been waiting for the summons brought a tray on which there was writing paper, an inkpot and a quill pen.

It was set down in front of Vita.

She reluctantly picked up the pen.

She had tried her best, she thought desperately, and failed!

The ink was rather thin, but gave a legible result and, when she had finished, she handed the letter to the Sheikh so that he could read what she had written.

> *"Dear Cousin Jane,*
>
> *You will not remember me, but my father, General Sir George Ashford, and my mother have spoken of you so often that I had a great desire to meet you when I was visiting Naples.*
>
> *Accordingly I came to Damascus, only to find that you had left for the desert.*
>
> *Mrs. Burton kindly arranged a caravan for me so that I could join you, but the Courier she employed, who was a Mezrab, was prevented from bringing me to you by Sheikh Shaa-lan El Hassein and I was tricked into becoming his prisoner.*
>
> *He has ordered me to write this letter to you asking you to come to my rescue.*
>
> *I am deeply upset and humiliated that I should have been used in this manner merely to cause trouble between his tribe and yours and I can only ask for your forgiveness.*
>
> *Please believe me when I assure you that I would not have had this happen for all the world.*
>
> *Yours unhappily,*
> *Vita Ashford."*

The Sheikh read it through with a swiftness that surprised Vita.

He must, she thought, be very proficient in English to be able to absorb the letter so quickly.

Then he folded it and, rising to his feet, said,

"This will be sent at once. It will be in your cousin's hands soon after dawn."

"Then they are not far from here?" Vita questioned.

"Not very far," he replied, "but much too far for you to walk."

She did not reply and he went on,

"You may now go to bed. I hope you will sleep well and in the morning, if it pleases you, I will show you my horses before they are damaged by war!"

"I would like that," Vita answered.

She rose to her feet and stood for a moment looking up at him.

He seemed very tall in the low-ceilinged tent.

"Good night," he said, "and may I commend you for your courage? I would not have believed it possible for any woman to have retained her sense of humour in such circumstances."

"Perhaps you don't give the poor things a chance to prove they have one!" Vita flashed.

The Sheikh gave a short laugh almost as if he could not help himself.

Then he said in a different tone from the one he had used before,

"You have done enough fighting for today. Go to bed, Miss Ashford, and remember, after all, it is *Insha'Allah*."

Chapter Five

The sounds of the camp rising early awakened Vita, who lay listening to the chatter of voices, the bleating of the goats and lambs being moved out to pasture and the laughter of the children.

After a while she rose and dressed, putting on her riding habit since the Sheikh had promised to show her his horses.

She was not certain whether he would let her ride them. At the same time it was what she wanted to do and, besides, she knew she had a great deal more to learn about Arabian thoroughbreds.

She walked into the outer tent and immediately a slave hurried to bring her coffee, freshly baked bread, although it was so early in the morning, and a big pat of butter, which had been made out of goat's or sheep's milk.

She knew that camel's milk was never used for this purpose and that making butter was one of the many tasks of the women of the tribe.

They were also entirely responsible for driving the sheep and cattle out to pasture. In fact the men thought it would be degrading for themselves to take part in the herding, just as they believed it was the women's job to fetch water from the well, however far it might be from their tents.

Vita especially enjoyed the delicious coffee, which she felt was an extravagance of the Sheikh's and that most Bedouins did not drink such an expensive blend except on special occasions.

She then rose from the *roffe* to go to the opening of the tent.

At that moment the Sheikh appeared.

He had already been riding, for he carried a short whip in his hand and wore the yellow leather boots that she had noticed the first time she had seen him on the quay.

"You are rested?" he asked.

"Yes, thank you," she replied, "and I am longing to see your horses, as you promised me.

He smiled at her enthusiasm and said,

"Come along. I have had them driven outside here so you will not have far to walk."

When Vita stepped from the tent, she drew in her breath appreciatively at what she saw.

She wished that her father was with her, for there were more than three hundred horses all gathered together.

She could not help thinking that any English breeder would give a great deal to be where she was at this very moment.

"I gather from the way you berated me when we first met," the Sheikh said, "that you have some knowledge of horses."

"My father has a big stable," Vita answered, "but I doubt if he has anything in it as fine as these."

She walked towards the horses and realised that Signor Dira had been right when he had told her how tame and affectionate the Arabians were.

The mares appeared to recognise the Sheikh and followed him, nuzzling against him and he had literally to push them aside to show Vita the ones he particularly wanted her to notice.

"When I saw the *djerid*," Vita said, "I realised how fast Arabians can go."

"We have no regular races," the Sheikh replied, "so it is difficult for us to assess the speed of an Arabian until he is sold to a European. But, as we are more interested in war, it is rather a question of endurance than of speed as to how we rate the best animal."

As he mentioned the war, Vita could not help looking over her shoulder towards the horizon.

It was far too soon for there to be yet any sign of the Mezrabs, but she knew that she was dreading the moment when the two tribes would fight over her and men would die needlessly and horses be wounded.

Because the thought of it made her nervous and unhappy she tried to concentrate on the horses the Sheikh was showing her.

"This is a Kehilan" he said. "I think the breed must have received their name from the black marks they have round their eyes. The markings give them the appearance of being painted with kohl like an Arabian woman."

The horse was very fine-looking and Vita patted his neck before the Sheikh pointed out another.

"This is a Kochlani," he said, "which are bred solely for riding. It is said they derive their origins from King Solomon's studs. Whether this is true or not, they have the greatest endurance and can bear the longest fatigue of any Arabian."

They moved on looking at horse after horse and the Sheikh told Vita what she knew already, that the Bedouin never used a bit or bridle of any sort on a horse, but instead a halter with a fine chain passing round the nose.

"I noticed that most of the men in the *djerid* rode in that manner," she said, "and it amazed me how they could control their horses so easily and effectively."

"I think perhaps it is because our animals are gentle and without vice," the Sheikh replied. "They have none of the viciousness of the European animals."

He paused and then said with a twist of his lips,

"That might also apply to people."

He turned away before Vita could say anything, but she wondered who it was that had upset him and caused him to be so bitter.

Then she remembered how he had uttered the name 'Elaine' when he held her down on the *roffe* and she found herself wondering who Elaine was and of what nationality.

The Sheikh had spoken in English, so it was easy to suppose that Elaine, whoever she might be, was of the same nationality as herself.

It would account, Vita thought, for the hostility in his eyes when he had first looked at her.

But once again she told herself that she was being imaginative and was making a Fairy story out of something that might have a quite simple explanation.

"How did it happen that there is such a specially fine breed of horses in Syria?" Vita asked.

"There is a legend that they are descended from the five mares of Solomon," the Sheikh replied. "But few Arabs believe it. What we do know is that our horses have a strain that is incomparable anywhere else in the world!"

"We in England admit that," Vita said.

She paused and then said a little tentatively,

"I would like to buy one of your horses."

"They are not for sale," the Sheikh replied sharply and walked on as if the subject was finished and he did not wish to refer to it again.

But Vita was sure that he had not told the truth.

She had been told that all the tribes sold their horses to make money and it was obvious from the presence of the Sheyfi stallion on board the Steamship with her that the Sheikh had sold to the Royal stable in Italy.

What he was really saying, she thought, was that he did not wish to sell to her and she wondered why he should still feel so aggressive towards her.

While he was talking about the horses he had seemed quite friendly and she might have been not a prisoner but an honoured guest whom he was showing round.

But now she had upset him in some way and she felt that he was the most unpredictable man that one could possibly imagine.

Almost as if he regretted his disagreeableness, the Sheikh signalled to a man to bring him a very beautiful white mare.

She was perhaps the most perfect horse that Vita had ever seen, pure white in colour with kohl patches round her eyes and a very strange nose marked with black.

Her ears were long like a hind's and her eyes were full and soft.

"She is lovely!" Vita exclaimed.

"She is a Hamdani," the Sheikh explained, "a very uncommon breed both amongst the Aeneze and our own people."

He saw the admiration in Vita's face and asked,

"Would you like to ride her?"

"You know I would!" Vita cried.

On the Sheikh's instructions, a side saddle was placed on the mare's back and he lifted Vita onto it.

She had been expecting him to wait for one of the servants to lock his hands in the usual manner so that she could mount herself.

It gave her a strange feeling when she felt the Sheikh's strong hands on either side of her small waist as he swung her up in the air.

The mare, whose name was Sherifa, responded to her touch and Vita rode through the grazing herd, feeling that she had never known before what it was to be on a truly magnificent horse until this moment.

Almost immediately Sherifa moved into a gallop and for a moment Vita thought that she was alone, until she heard the thudding of hoofs behind her and a moment later the Sheikh was at her side on a black stallion.

She looked round at him and he said with a smile on his lips,

"I am not offering an easy way for you to escape, so do *not* try it!"

"Actually I had not thought of such a thing," Vita said truthfully.

But now that he had put the idea into her mind, she began to plan.

If she could reach Sherifa when no one was looking, it would be easy to get away from the camp and perhaps ride to meet the Mezrabs before they actually attacked.

She was thinking as they galloped on for some time, then the Sheikh put out his hand, still at full gallop, and, taking Sherifa's bridle, turned her round to face back in the direction of the camp.

"Are you afraid that we might meet your enemies on their way to rescue me?" Vita asked lightly.

"They will take longer than this to prepare themselves," the Sheikh replied.

At the same time, almost instinctively, he looked towards the East and Vita knew without being told the direction that the Mezrabs would come from.

They galloped back to the camp and, as she drew the mare to a standstill, she said,

"Thank you! I have never enjoyed a ride more! Sherifa is perfect!"

"I am glad you think so," the Sheikh replied.

"I would like to feed her myself."

The Sheikh gave an order and one of his men ran to bring back a bowl filled with some strange-looking pieces of food, which Sherifa obviously found extremely delectable.

The food was soon finished, but the mare followed them back to the tent, which was just what Vita wanted her to do.

As she patted and talked to Sherifa, the mare nuzzled against her and would have followed her into the tent itself if the Sheikh had not shooed her away.

The morning had passed so quickly and so enjoyably that Vita was quite surprised to find that it was midday and that a meal was waiting for them.

This time they ate *kemmdye*, which the Sheikh said was a favourite food of the Arabs and was a kind of truffle that grew in the desert.

"It closely resembles the true truffle that the French prize so highly," he said. "We have three different species here, the red, the black and the white."

The *kemmdye* were boiled in milk until they formed a paste over which melted butter had been poured.

Vita tasted hers rather tentatively and found that it was in fact very pleasant to eat. She could understand it being a very convenient food, being available in the most inaccessible spots in the desert.

There were small eggs, which Vita learnt had been laid by quails and plenty of the freshly baked *fisre* with butter.

When they had finished eating, the Sheikh said,

"Now I suggest you rest. It is very hot at this time of the day."

"I found that yesterday," Vita replied, "and I was glad when we reached an oasis."

"Then go and lie down," the Sheikh insisted. "If we are not at war by nightfall, I will entertain you with some Arabic music."

"I would like that," Vita said and she smiled at him as she went to her own part of the tent.

She had, however, while she was riding, already made her plans and, when she peeped through the flap of her tent, she saw as she expected that Sherifa was outside, still hoping for more attention.

The Bedouin woman who had attended her the night before came to help her take off her riding habit.

When she had done so, Vita made clear, partly in sign language and partly in the words she had learnt, that she wanted to try on a Bedouin dress and also a *burnouse*.

The woman looked surprised, but then she giggled and, like women of every race all the world over, was only too delighted to take part in the eternal feminine game of dressing up.

She hurried away and came back with several other women.

They had understood that Vita wanted to see what they wore and they brought their long cotton gowns in blue, brown and black. They also showed her their jewellery and a white *burnouse* which all Arabs of either sex cover themselves with when travelling.

They showed Vita the kerchief called a *shauber*, which the young women wore of red and the older of black. She handled the silver rings, which they could wear both in their ears and through their noses and the bracelets and anklets that made a musical sound as they moved.

As she admired everything, she noticed that, while all the women were trying to attract her attention, one stood apart and merely looked at her in a sulky almost insolent manner.

Vita had not noticed her when she first came into the tent, but now she saw that she was very beautiful, young, with almost perfect features and her head set gracefully on her long neck.

Her skin was rather fairer than that of the other women and she thought that she must be of the tribe of El Hadedyein whose women were celebrated for the fairness of their skins.

Looking at her Vita realised that she wore more jewellery than the others and that some of it was in fact quite valuable.

She spoke to the girl, as she was little more, but she did not reply. Instead she looked at Vita in a sullen manner, then turned and went from the tent.

Vita looked after her in surprise and then realised that the other women were giving each other knowing glances and giggling a little.

"Zabla is jealous," one woman said in Arabic.

It was then that Vita understood.

This girl was the Sheikh's woman and was obviously annoyed by her intrusion into the camp.

Vita could understand his interest in her since she was so genuinely beautiful.

But her behaviour was somehow perturbing and she signalled to the women that she wished to rest.

She did, however, ask if they would leave a gown and a *burnouse* for her to try on later.

They laid them on the ground and insisted on leaving some of their jewellery as well, including a number of glass bangles, which Vita gathered were particularly popular with them.

Waiting until they had gone, she rose from the bed she had lain down on in their presence and started to dress herself again.

As she did so, she realised that the camp was very quiet and she was certain that everyone, except perhaps some of the men on duty as sentries, would be resting.

She put on the skirt of her riding habit and the white blouse that went under her jacket.

Then she covered herself in the white *burnouse*, pulling the hood low over her face.

She knew it would be hard at a distance for anyone to know whether she was a man or a woman.

Then very very cautiously she undid the flap of her tent, which had been closed against the afternoon heat and stepped outside.

Sherifa was perhaps twenty yards away. Vita did not have to make a sound as the mare seemed to know instinctively that she was there and came towards her.

She still wore the bridle and the saddle that had been put on her in the morning and Vita knew that the Arabs were very slovenly about unsaddling their horses.

In fact it was quite usual, Signor Dira had told her, for the saddle once on a horse never to be taken from its back.

"In the wintertime," he said, "a sackcloth is thrown over the saddle, but in the summer the horse stands exposed to the midday sun.

"Surely that is not good for the animal?" Vita had asked sharply.

"Arabian horses are tough," the *signore* had replied, "and their saddles are not like European ones. They are soft sheepskin pads without stirrups."

For Vita, however, the Sheikh had provided a leather side saddle and Sherifa was wearing a bridle.

It was a very light one, but even so Vita thought only a very good-tempered horse would submit to being bridled after always having been ridden with a halter.

But it was a great convenience to her at this moment.

She waited until Sherifa was at her side, nuzzling against her as she had done before. Then swiftly she mounted the mare and turned her head towards the desert.

They had been in the shadow of the tent which, being to the West of the camp and standing by itself, was, Vita thought, sure to be out of sight of the men on guard.

But now, as she started off at full gallop, she knew that she would be seen and wondered how long it would be before she was followed.

She was quite certain, however, that Sherifa would be able to outpace any other horse and it would take some time for anyone who had seen her to go and raise the alarm. They would also have to ask the Sheikh's permission to follow her.

She hoped too that, since she was wearing the *burnouse*, they would not at first realise that it was their prisoner who had escaped.

They might even think it was a man carrying a message from the Sheikh himself.

All sorts of thoughts and ideas ran through her mind, even the idea that someone might shoot her. But nothing happened and, after she had gone for well over a mile, she looked back and saw that she was not being followed.

With a leap of her heart she thought that perhaps she really had escaped and now she turned Sherifa's face in an Eastward direction and left the mare to carry her away as fast as she could.

They had galloped for nearly an hour before the mare began to slacken pace and Vita realised how extremely hot she was.

She pushed back the hood from her head, but the burning rays of the sun made her hotter still and, afraid of getting sunstroke, she replaced it.

At the same time she knew that such a long gallop in the hottest part of the day had taken its toll of both herself and Sherifa.

Now they moved more slowly and Vita hoped that she would see an oasis or some shade.

It would be unwise to linger for long in case those who must be following her should catch up with her, but a respite was almost essential.

She was quite certain that the Sheikh would not let her go easily.

As he had said, she was the 'trump card', and, if he really wished to fight the Mezrabs, she had provided him with an incentive.

'Why can he not content himself with the beautiful Zabla instead of wanting to make war?' she asked herself.

She wondered if he really loved Zabla and then she told herself that he did not appear like a man who loved anyone.

Most of the Arabs were smiling, happy-looking young men who seemed to enjoy life and who, with their flashing, sparkling dark eyes, Vita could imagine would find plenty of lovemaking to keep themselves amused and interested.

But the Sheikh was different.

There was not only a reserve about him, there was also the clear suggestion that hidden deeply in him was some inherent hatred.

'It is because of Elaine that he hates me!' Vita told herself.

Then she thought that Zabla, so slim and lovely, should be ample compensation for any Elaine, whatever she had meant to him.

The thought of love brought Vita back to her own problems.

Somehow she had to reach Cousin Jane and ask her what she should do about Lord Bantham.

Whatever was happening now, sooner or later she would be faced with marrying a man she disliked or else incur the anger of her father and the punishments that he could inflict so subtly.

She could not help being a little frightened of what he would say about her latest escapade, but with an almost childlike trust she told herself that Cousin Jane would find a solution.

Yet what it could possibly be, she had no idea!

On and on she rode and at times the heat was almost unbearable. She knew that only a really fine animal like Sherifa could endure such a punishing ride.

Again and again Vita looked behind her, but there was still no sign of pursuit and after a while she told herself that the Sheikh was glad to be rid of her.

'Perhaps secretly he found me a nuisance and an encumbrance,' she thought. 'If he makes no effort to pursue me, then I can prevent the Mezrabs from going to war on my behalf and the Sheikh will just forget me.'

Strangely enough she could not help wishing that she had grown to know him a little better.

There had been a warmth and something very human about him when he had been showing her his horses.

There was no doubt that he loved them and that he was extremely knowledgeable on the subject of their breeding.

There was so much more she wanted to ask him, so much she wanted to learn.

'I shall never have such an opportunity again,' she thought sadly. 'When I return to England, I shall have to be content with people talking about Godolphin Arabian and Darby Arabian and they will never believe that I have seen, patted and ridden even finer breeds here in Syria.'

It was very annoying that the Sheikh would not sell her a horse to take back to England with her.

She was sure that it would be easy to placate her father's anger if she presented him with a mare like Sherifa or a stallion of the Kehilan breed.

Perhaps the Aeneze, when she reached them, would be more amenable, she hoped.

The heat of the day abated a little as the hours went by, but riding through them had left Vita depleted and more exhausted than she had ever felt before.

She thought that by now she ought to have had a sight of the Mezrabs if they were coming from the direction that the Sheikh had indicated, but there was nothing except desert all around her and ahead.

The only signs of life were the animals and birds she had seen on her journey from Damascus.

The storks with their wide wingspan flapped into the air at her approach. There were clouds of kattahs, covies of partridges and occasionally an eagle circling in the sky.

On and on she rode and now Vita began to feel intolerably weary and she knew that Sherifa was exhausted too.

Her lips were dry and her throat hurt, so that she felt it would be difficult to speak even when she did arrive at her cousin's camp.

Then suddenly she saw a dark patch in the wilderness ahead and she was sure that it was an oasis!

Sherifa must have seen it too for she quickened her pace.

It was an oasis and, as Sherifa moved into the shade of the palms, Vita swung herself down from the saddle.

For a moment she felt so weak that her legs seemed to buckle beneath her and she half fell to the ground.

Then she saw that Sherifa was standing dejectedly still, her tongue hanging out, and she realised that the horse was as thirsty as she was.

With an effort Vita pulled herself to her feet and walked towards the well. She bent over the roughly-bricked surround and saw that the water was very far away.

There was the usual pail attached to a long rope beside the well and Vita knew that she must let it down, fill it with water and draw it up so that both she and Sherifa could drink.

She realised of course that it was not going to be as easy for her to bring water to the surface as it would have been for a man.

If she filled the pail too full, it would be too heavy for her and she would be unable to pull it up.

She looked at the rough rope tentatively, knowing it would be painful for her hands. At the same time both she and Sherifa were desperately in need of water.

The mare had drawn nearer to her as she stood at the well and now nuzzled her nose against her arm as if urging her to do what was necessary.

Vita undid the *burnouse* and threw it to the ground.

It had kept out the rays of the sun, but it had also made her very hot and she thought that what she would like above all else was to bathe in the well herself, to have a cold bath.

"Why could we not have found an oasis with a pool instead of a well?" she asked Sherifa and her voice was only a croak, so strange that she could hardly recognise it.

She picked up the bucket and let it down slowly.

The rope was knotted every few feet to prevent it slipping, but even so, as Vita had anticipated, it was very hard on her hands.

Down and down it went and she thought that it would never reach the bottom, until she felt it rest on top of the water, then sink slowly.

Quickly she started to pull it up and then she realised that she was too late!

The pail was full and, although she strained with all her might, she knew that it was too heavy for her to haul up.

She pulled and pulled and then frantically she tried to shake the rope and spill out some of the water in the pail. But it was so far down from the top that it was impossible.

By moving the pail about she only filled it fuller. Now, she thought desperately, she would never be able to lift it.

Still Vita went on trying and, as if Sherifa was growing impatient, she kept nuzzling her arm and her back.

Finally the rope in her hands was so painful that inadvertently Vita let it go and now it ran out the full length from where it was attached by an iron ring to the stone surround of the well.

The pail must have dropped another three or four feet and Vita knew despairingly that she would never be able to raise it from the bottom.

She looked down into the well again.

It was dark, cool and almost uncannily quiet and she thought that if she fell in no one would ever know.

She would never be found!

With a sudden burst of energy born of despair, she grasped hold of the rope and tried once again to lift the pail, but it was too heavy.

"I cannot – Sherifa!" she cried despairingly. "I cannot – move it!"

Her voice broke on the words and now tears of frustration ran down her cheeks.

"It is – impossible!" she cried. "Oh, Sherifa – I am – so sorry!"

"I think you need my help," a voice remarked.

Vita started violently and turned round from the well.

Standing under the trees a little way from her stood the Sheikh!

She stared at him incredulously and then without thought, without reason, merely because she was so glad that he was there, she ran towards him.

She was not quite certain how it happened, but suddenly she had reached him and he put his arms round her.

She looked up at him, his hold tightened and his lips came down on hers.

For the moment she was not even surprised.

It was inevitable – Fate – something that had to happen.

Then, as his mouth held hers captive, something wild and wonderful that she had never felt or known before swept through Vita.

She had never dreamt, she thought, that a kiss would be like this. So incredible, so glorious that the whole world stood still.

Yet she knew it was everything that she had longed for, desired and sought until this moment.

The Sheikh held her closer and still closer.

She felt as if the trees bent their branches to protect them and they were in a cool green place that was not part of this world, but was a secret Heaven of their own.

Then, when her whole body was pulsating with the wonder of his lips and she felt as if she was a part of him and no longer herself, the Sheikh raised his head.

He looked down at her, at her eyes wide and shining, at her lips parted from the touch of his.

Then deliberately, as if with a superhuman effort, he took his arms from her and walked towards the well.

He did not look back, but taking hold of the rope started to pull up the bucket of water.

Vita watched him, unable to move, unable for the moment even to breathe.

He had kissed her and her heart had become his at the touch of his lips.

She felt herself still quivering with the wonder of it.

The Sheikh lifted the pail onto the surrounding stones and, pushing Sherifa aside to make her wait, he looked towards Vita.

Slowly, as if it was almost impossible to put one foot in front of another, she went towards him, her eyes on his face, until she reached him.

She stood looking up at him, bemused to the point when she could no longer remember that she was thirsty or in need of anything except him.

"Drink!" he ordered.

With an effort she looked towards the bucket, saw it brimming over with water and put her face down into it.

She drank thirstily and then rinsed her face in the cool clear water and felt as if it washed away so much more than the dust of the desert.

She raised her head and the Sheikh gave her a white linen handkerchief to dry her face with.

As she did so, he set the pail down in front of Sherifa who gulped the water down noisily.

Vita looked at the Sheikh.

For a moment she thought that he was about to turn away from her.

Then suddenly he pulled her roughly into his arms and held her crushingly against him.

He kissed her again and this time his kisses were fiercer, more demanding, more passionate, and yet she was not afraid.

She felt as if her whole heart and body leapt towards him to become a part of him, so that her heart beat with his and she was no longer herself but surrendered her whole being into his keeping.

He kissed her lips, her eyes, her cheeks, then again her mouth, and she felt the fire of his kisses burning through her.

Then, as suddenly as he had drawn her close to him, he picked her up in his arms and set her on Sherifa's back.

The *burnouse* was lying on the ground where she had thrown it. He laid it on the saddle of his own horse that had come, while he was kissing her, to drink what water was left in the bucket after Sherifa had finished.

"H-how – did you – find me?" Vita asked unsteadily.

They were the first words she had been able to speak since she had found him in the oasis.

"I have followed you all the afternoon," he answered.

"Why did you not overtake me sooner?"

He smiled.

"We are not far from home. You did not know that in the desert, both animals and humans always move in a circle. Sherifa was bringing you back!"

"I am – glad!" Vita said softly, her eyes on his.

For a moment he was still and she had the feeling that he was debating whether he would kiss her again.

Then he swung himself into the saddle.

"You are tired," he said. "Let's return."

As if the horses were refreshed by the water they had drunk at the oasis and also knew that home was not far away, they moved into a gallop. It was almost as swift and spontaneous as when Vita had left the camp.

She was content not to talk, but there was a great deal she wanted to say, so much she wanted to hear.

Yet for the moment it was a happiness beyond expression to be beside the Sheikh and to still feel his lips against hers.

'This is love!' she thought. 'This is what Cousin Jane found in the desert and I have found it too!'

She knew the emotion he aroused in her was very unlike anything she had ever imagined she might feel for an Englishman and certainly not for Lord Bantham.

It was something wild and primitive and yet at the same time spiritual and wonderful.

She had known when he kissed her that this was the answer to her problems, as Cousin Jane could never have answered them.

It was love she had wanted and love she had found when she least expected it.

It was Fate – it was *Insha'Allah* that had been with them both since the beginning of time.

'We have found each other across eternity!' Vita told herself and felt an inexplicable gladness.

She had been able to break through the conventions and everything else that might have kept her apart from the man who was meant for her.

For the moment she could not even begin to think of what it might mean in the future if she told her parents that she intended to stay in the desert with a man who was a Bedouin, a man who had not even said that he loved her or wished to marry her.

These things would somehow sort themselves out.

All that mattered at the moment was that she loved him and they had found each other.

'I love him! *I love him!*' Vita thought as their horses thundered on over the soft ground and quicker than she believed it possible she saw the black tents ahead of them.

They dismounted and Vita walked into the tent.

The Sheikh followed her and she wanted once again to throw herself into his arms and to feel his lips on hers.

But there were servants present and, because there was nothing else she could do, Vita went to her own part of the tent where the women who looked after her were waiting.

Now to her relief when she had undressed the women brought in a large tin bath and filled it with jugs of cool water.

There was jasmine to scent it and, when she had bathed, the women enveloped her in white towels and helped her to dry herself.

Because her hair was full of sand she washed that too and they rubbed it dry, exclaiming as they did so over the soft silky texture of it, so unlike their much coarser hair.

They brought Vita coffee and pieces of *heneyne*.

But she was no longer hungry or thirsty.

She was aglow with a strange unbelievable happiness and all she wanted was to be with the Sheikh.

She chose the prettiest of her gowns and, having brought some semblance of order to her hair, which, after being washed, was curling almost riotously round her head, she walked into the outer tent.

She found it hard to breathe because she was so excited at the thought of seeing the Sheikh again.

Her eyes lit up at the sight of him, but, when she would have run towards him, she realised with a little throb of disappointment that he was not alone.

There was a young man seated beside him on the *roffe*, wearing a gold embroidered *abbas*, whose dark eyes showed an unmistakable expression of admiration.

"Miss Ashford, may I present Hedjaz El Hassein?" the Sheikh asked. "Hedjaz, this is Miss Vita Ashford, who I have spoken to you about."

Vita curtseyed and Hedjaz El Hassein rose and bowed.

"Hedjaz has just arrived from Paris where he has been attending the Sorbonne," the Sheikh said in French. "He regretfully speaks very little English, but his French is extremely good,'"

He paused to add a little dryly,

"It ought to be, after four years of tuition!"

"I am enchanted, *mademoiselle*, to make your acquaintance!" Hedjaz El Hassein said. "I have heard how brave you have been in very exceptional circumstances."

"*Merci, monsieur*," Vita replied.

She looked at the Sheikh and then seated herself beside him on the *roffe*.

She felt it very disappointing that this young man should have arrived at this particular moment when she wanted so desperately to be alone with the man who had kissed her.

But Hedjaz obviously belonged to the tribe and there was a great deal he wanted to know about the people and affairs she knew nothing about.

She was therefore obliged to sit silent listening to the two men talking to each other.

Almost immediately dinner was brought in and, although she thought she was not hungry, she found in fact that she was very glad to have something to eat.

It took away much of her fatigue, although she was aware that she was actually very tired.

It had been a long day and apart from the exhaustion of her ride, there were the emotions she had experienced that also seemed somehow to have taken their toll of her strength.

Tonight instead of lamb they had gazelle, which was so young and so tender that it was even more delicious than the lamb had been.

When the great wooden dish containing it was brought in, Hedjaz laughed.

"I have almost forgotten how to eat with my fingers," he said. "I think I shall have to introduce knives and forks to the camp. It would be more civilised.

"That is, of course, up to you," the Sheikh replied.

"What is more, I shall miss the French wines I have been enjoying," Hedjaz continued.

"That I should not advise as an innovation," the Sheikh said, "and anyway those of our followers who are Mohammedans would certainly not approve of it!"

"Nor would the rest," Hedjaz said, "so I presume I shall have to suffer!"

"Nothing is perfect in this life!" the Sheikh remarked, "and perhaps a momentous sacrifice such as giving up wine will be compensated by other pleasures!"

He spoke sarcastically but Hedjaz laughed.

"You know full well I am glad to be back," he said. "There is so much I want to do, so many people I want to see!"

He looked at Vita.

"Your cousin, *mademoiselle*, the Honourable Jane Digby, is very much admired in Syria."

"You have met her?" Vita asked.

"I have seen her in Damascus where she is 'a *grande dame*!' he replied, "but in the desert she is an Amazon and the Bedouins worship her!"

Hedjaz turned to the Sheikh.

"Is Fares El Meziad still pursuing the lovely *Sitt?*" he asked.

"I believe so," the Sheikh replied stiffly.

"Who is that?" Vita asked curiously.

"Sheikh Fares is a puissant Prince who owns enormous territories," Hedjaz replied. "He has coveted Sheikh Medjuel's fascinating wife ever since they married and has pursued her relentlessly."

"He has made himself the laughing stock of the Bedouin world!" the Sheikh interposed.

"Who shall blame him when the Honourable Jane is so beautiful?" Hedjaz asked lightly and added, "like her cousin!"

He looked at Vita eloquently as he spoke.

"*Merci, monsieur,*" she said demurely.

The Sheikh made an impatient movement.

She glanced at him and saw an expression of anger in his face and a fire burning in his dark eyes.

He was jealous!

Vita felt herself thrill with the knowledge that he cared.

Hedjaz rose to his feet saying,

"Now that we have finished dinner, I must go and find my mother."

"I am sure that she is awaiting your arrival with great impatience," the Sheikh replied.

"I expect too she has a list of wives for my inspection," Hedjaz remarked, "and she will never understand that I have other ideas on that subject as well!"

He glanced at Vita as he spoke and she knew without his putting it into words that he had found the women he had met in France attractive and desirable.

It made her think of Zabla and she was sure that she was waiting for the Sheikh somewhere in the forest of tents behind them.

For the first time in her life Vita felt a painful stab of jealousy herself.

Zabla was so beautiful, her figure so perfect and there was a grace about her, she thought, that could not be emulated by any European.

Suddenly she felt unsure of her innermost conviction that the Sheikh and she meant something special to each other.

The knowledge of it had glowed like a jewel within her as they had ridden back from the oasis.

All the time she was washing and dressing it had been there, almost as if she held within herself a talisman of her love.

Now she was afraid.

She looked at him uncertainly but now, as Hedjaz said goodnight, she thought that the moment had come when she could tell him of her love.

The young man bowed to the Sheikh and then in the French fashion he bowed to Vita and lifted her hand to his lips.

"*Bonsoir, mademoiselle*," he said. "We shall meet tomorrow."

"*Bonsoir, monsieur.*"

He gave her a very eloquent look of admiration and then left the tent leaving Vita and the Sheikh alone.

For a moment there was a strange unnatural silence.

Then Vita moved to lay her cheek against his shoulder.

"I love – you!" she said softly.

Just for a moment the Sheikh was still and then abruptly he rose to his feet.

"You leave at dawn!" he said harshly. "I am sending you to Sheikh Medjuel El Mezrab!"

Chapter Six

There was silence and the Sheikh stared out into the darkness of the desert where the sky was rapidly being filled with the twinkling brilliance of stars.

Then behind him a small lost little voice said,

"You mean – you do not – want me?"

There was a pause before the Sheikh turned round.

Vita was standing in the centre of the tent and the expression on her face turned towards him was very young and pathetic, the look of a child who has been hurt when she least expected it.

For a moment the Sheikh stared at her.

Then he said sharply,

"No, of course I want you! You know I want you, but you have to forget everything that happened today."

"Why? *Why?*" Vita asked.

"Because I have nothing to offer you," he said.

Once again, as if he could not bear to look at her, he turned to the right.

She moved a little nearer to him.

"Why can I – not – stay with you?" she asked in a voice little above a whisper.

"Because I shall not be here."

His voice seemed unnaturally loud.

"But why are you – going away?" Vita asked. "I don't – understand."

Without looking at her, he walked across the tent to the *roffe*.

"Come and sit down," he said. "I will give you an explanation."

She moved slowly towards him.

But sensing his wish, she did not sit beside him, but sat a little apart, turning sideways so that her face was turned towards his.

"The young man you have just met," he said after a moment, "is the Sheikh of the El Hasseins."

"I thought that *you* were the Sheikh and that the Bedouins could not – depose their – Sheikhs," Vita said hesitatingly.

"I was merely acting on Hedjaz's behalf until he grew up," the Sheikh said. "Now he will take over the tribe."

"But surely you can stay with them too?" Vita asked.

"No, I must go away," he answered. "My usefulness here is finished."

"Then if you have – to go away," Vita said tentatively, "why can I not – go with – you?"

There was a pleading note in her voice and unconsciously she moved a little nearer to him.

"Do you suppose I don't wish that was possible?" he asked harshly.

He turned his head to look at her and then rose to his feet.

"For God's sake, don't look at me like that!" he said. "If you do so, you will find that where you are concerned I am not very civilised."

Vita turned her flower-like face up to his.

"*I love – you*!" she sighed.

The words seemed to tremble between them, until, as if he could not help it, the Sheikh bent down and pulled her into his arms.

He held her crushingly against him and then he was kissing her wildly!

Kissing her with lips that hurt and bruised the softness of her skin, but still evoked a burning fire within her so that she felt as if a wild and wonderful flame carried them both into the starlit sky.

Only when it seemed impossible to breathe and she was quivering against him with the ecstasy of the emotions he aroused in her, did he throw her from him so that she staggered and if it had not been for the *roffe* would have fallen to the ground.

"I told you not to tempt me!" he said. "Go away and forget that we have ever met."

"You know it – would be – impossible for me to do that," Vita whispered.

She drew in her breath and added,

"I want to – stay with you. I love – you! I cannot live – without you!"

"You are very young," the Sheikh said as if speaking to himself. "You will forget, of course you will forget."

"I don't believe that love has – anything to do with – age," Vita said. "I came to Syria because I could not find an – answer to a problem – but now I have – found it. The answer is – *you*!"

"That is not the truth!" he contradicted.

"Why not?" she asked.

"Because," he said, "I am a man without a background, without roots, with nothing to offer you except myself, and that is not enough."

"The desert is a big place. There will be room for us somewhere," Vita suggested.

"I am not a Bedouin!"

He saw the astonishment in Vita's eyes and added,

"If you want the truth, I am Spanish!"

"Spanish?" Vita murmured.

She had never imagined that he might not be what he seemed.

"I will tell you the whole story," he said in a weary voice, "but keep away from me. I will not answer for the consequences if you tempt me again."

He spoke so sternly that Vita made no effort to draw closer to him as he seated himself as far away from her as he could on the *roffe*.

"I lived in Spain until I was nineteen," he began. "Then my father sent me to the Sorbonne in Paris to finish my education. It was there I met Othman El Hassein, the oldest son of the Sheikh of this tribe and he became my greatest friend."

He paused as if he was remembering how much that friendship had meant before he went on,

"Othman and I did everything together. We were very much alike and he enthralled me with his stories of the Bedouins and of Syria."

"I can – understand that," Vita murmured, thinking how thrilling she too had found the desert.

"In my last year at the Sorbonne when I was twenty-one," the Sheikh said, "I fell in love with an English girl."

"Elaine!" Vita ejaculated.

The Sheikh looked at her in astonishment.

"How do you know her name?"

"You called me – Elaine when we were – struggling," she answered faintly, the blood rising in her cheeks.

"Like you she had fair hair," the Sheikh said, "which is why I have loathed all Englishwomen ever since I knew her."

"What did she do that made you so – unhappy?"

"She promised to marry me," the Sheikh replied. "I went back to Spain to ask the permission of my father and because he refused we fought bitterly. He told me that Elaine, who was an actress, was only interested in my money. I swore that she loved me for myself."

"She – told you so?" Vita asked.

It hurt her physically to think of the Sheikh and Elaine loving each other.

"Most emphatically!" the Sheikh answered. "But I found that I was like every other fool who believes what a woman says."

He looked at Vita as he spoke, saw the hurt in her eyes and said quickly,

"Not you, my precious love, but other women. All the women I have ever known until now."

Vita drew in her breath and then she said quickly,

"Finish telling me about – Elaine."

"I returned to Paris," the Sheikh went on, "certain that despite the fact that my father had cut me off without a penny it would make no difference where Elaine was concerned. I decided I would find work, any work as long as we could be married and be together."

His voice died away and after a moment Vita asked,

"What happened?"

"She laughed at me. My father was right! She was not interested in a penniless young man, only a rich one!"

"How cruel! How heartless!" Vita exclaimed. "What did you do?"

"Because I was so upset, Othman persuaded me to return home with him and stay with his tribe."

"So you accepted his invitation!"

"We set off together. I had already learnt Arabic and Othman had told me so much about his people that I felt as if I too was going home."

The Sheikh paused.

Then he said with a note of pain that was inescapable,

"Othman contracted a virulent fever in Marseilles and died of a fever on the voyage,"

"How terrible! How distressing for you!" Vita cried.

"I arrived in Syria to find his tribe waiting for him," the Sheikh continued. "Tragedies never come singly."

"What had happened?"

"Othman's father had just died too. The tribe had no one to lead them except Hedjaz, a boy of fourteen."

"So you became the Sheikh!" Vita exclaimed.

"Because I resembled Othman, because I knew their history, could speak their language and already loved them, I consented to act as Regent for eight years until Hedjaz was old enough to take his rightful place at their head."

"And – now he has come – back," Vita said almost beneath her breath.

"He has been educated as his brother was. He is qualified to take his place with the more civilised Sheikhs who now control the Bedouin tribes and so I am out of a job!"

There was a bitter twist to his lips as the Sheikh finished speaking.

"I never imagined that you might not be a Bedouin," Vita said, "and I can understand why the tribe accepted you so readily."

"I am pure Spanish, except for an English grandmother," the Sheikh said. "But that does not make me anything at the moment but an impoverished homeless man."

He rose, as he spoke, to walk once again across the tent as if there was some inner restlessness in him that prevented him from keeping still.

Then, as he stood with his back to her, Vita said very quietly,

"I have – money, quite a – lot of it."

"You don't suppose that I would touch it?" the Sheikh asked angrily. "I have not sunk so low that I would take money from a woman. If I have nothing else left, I have my pride."

Vita gave a deep sigh.

She knew how proud the Spaniards were and she had known even as she spoke that he would find it unthinkable to accept any help from her.

And yet, she thought desperately, if she could not find a solution to his problem he would leave her and she might never see him again.

She rose to her feet to go to the opening of the tent and stand beside him.

"Please – listen to me," she pleaded.

"No!" he replied. "I have made up my mind and nothing you can say will change it! I will send you back to your cousin. It was madness for me to have prevented you from going to her in the first place."

"Why did you – do so?"

"Because," he answered, "you were the most beautiful woman I have ever seen and I told myself that I hated you!"

He gave a short laugh without any humour in it.

"I thought I was being so clever! Punishing you because you were English and needling Sheikh Medjuel into rescuing you, thereby causing a small war which would please the tribe."

"And when you – met me?" Vita asked.

"The moment you came into this tent," the Sheikh said in a deep voice, "I knew I wanted you. I knew that you were my Fate and what I felt for you was certainly not hatred. But I would not admit it to myself."

"Then – can you not – understand that we must – be together?" Vita asked.

"How? How can we be?" he asked bitterly. "Do you think I could drag you about the world with me, watching you suffer from the sordid circumstances of having no money, no position?"

"I am not interested in – either of those things," Vita said quickly.

"Only because you have never known the lack of them!" he retorted. "Can you not see that it would be a living hell to see you become disillusioned with me, to watch you having to perform menial tasks, to skimp and save and to know that nobody cared?"

"We could go – back to – England," Vita suggested.

"I can imagine how warmly your father would welcome me!" the Sheikh replied. "A penniless suitor, a fortune-hunter! A foreigner you picked up in the desert!"

He spoke so contemptuously that Vita gave a little cry.

"You are making everything – horrible and – ugly," she protested. "The love I have for you is so – beautiful that it is part of the – Divine."

He turned to look at her and the harshness faded from his face.

"Oh, my lovely one," he said. "You are so perfect, so different in every way from any other woman I have ever known. I adore your courage, your sense of humour, your purity and most of all the spirituality about you, so that I know it is the truth when you tell me that our love is Divine."

The caressing note in his voice made Vita's heart turn over in her breast.

Then, as she put out her hands towards him, he took them and kissed them, his lips hard and passionate as he turned them over and kissed the palms.

"I worship you!" he said. "And that is why I will not pull you down to my level. Go back to England, my lovely darling, and think sometimes of the man who will adore you all his life."

Vita's fingers tightened on his.

"I cannot – leave you!" she said and her voice broke on the words.

"We have no choice, my precious love."

Now there was a sadness about the Sheikh, which made what he said seem even more determined than when he had been violent.

Still holding Vita's hands he looked into her eyes.

"I dare not kiss you again," he said hoarsely. "If I did I should make you mine and then there would be no escape for either of us."

"That is – what I – want," Vita whispered breathlessly.

"It is because you are so perfect," he said, "because you are the woman I have dreamt of but never thought existed that I cannot spoil you. That is why, my dearest heart, you must forget."

"And will you be – able to – forget?"

"I shall try," he answered. "God knows I shall try!"

He kissed the palms of her hands again, hot, burning, demanding kisses that aroused a wild response within her so that she wanted the touch of his mouth on her lips more than she had ever wanted anything in her whole life.

Then he dropped her hands and walked from the tent out into the darkness and she knew helplessly that it would be futile to go after him.

She stood for a long time staring up at the starlit sky and feeling as if her heart would break.

Then, like an animal that must hide because it has been hurt, she went to her own part of the tent, undressed and climbed slowly into bed.

She lay with her face in the pillow feeling more desolate than she had thought it possible to feel.

She did not cry – she was past tears.

She only knew that the world was a great, empty, frightening place and she could not bear to contemplate the future.

"If only I could die!" she murmured at last.

Then slowly, bitterly, the tears came.

*

Three hours' ride away another woman was lying sleepless, looking up into the darkness of her tent.

Jane Digby El Mezrab had received Vita's letter soon after sunrise.

She was told that a lone rider had galloped into the camp, handed the letter to the first man he met and then galloped away to the West.

When the letter was handed to Jane, she had just said goodbye to her husband, Sheikh Medjuel, who, with two dozen members of the tribe, had gone shooting.

It was partly pleasure, partly business.

Partridges, quail, gazelles and an occasional wild boar were all needed as an alternative food to *kemmdye*.

At the same time eagles had been carrying off a number of the newly born lambs, obviously to feed their young. So it was plain that the nest must be discovered and destroyed.

Usually when Medjuel went shooting or hunting Jane went with him. But she had been suffering for the last few days from a cold and had decided to spend a quiet day in the camp.

She received Vita's letter with consternation and while she was still reading it, finding it difficult to believe that the information it contained could actually be the truth, another letter arrived from Damascus.

It was brought by one of the Mezrabs, who had remained behind when the tribe had left to look for pasturage.

The letter was from Isobel Burton and was extremely hysterical.

Mrs. Burton explained how Vita had come to ask her help and how she had engaged Yousef to escort her into the desert.

It was only after she had gone that Yousef arrived at the house to say that he had been held captive by men of Sheikh Shaa-lan El Hassein's tribe and that the man, Nasir, a Mezrab who was known to do anything for money, had escorted Vita in his place.

Isobel Burton went on,

"I cannot tell you how deeply the whole situation has upset me or how distressed I feel that your cousin should have been subjected to such an insult.

She is so young and so lovely that one cannot bear to think of her suffering in such circumstances.

She told me that your family think she is like you and it is indeed true, dear Jane, for she is a great beauty and must be a living replica of you at eighteen.

I can only hope that you and your husband will somehow rescue her from this terrible predicament and I assure you that I am praying that when you find Vita no harm will have come to her."

'A living replica of you at eighteen!'

Jane repeated the words to herself and was afraid, not for Vita but for herself.

After twelve years of being happily married to Medjuel she was desperately and incessantly jealous.

There was no obvious reason why she should doubt his love for her and yet Jane tortured herself and grew increasingly suspicious of her step-daughter-in-law, Ouadijid.

It did not make things any better that Sheikh Fares El Meziad, who had pursued her for years, was always insinuating that Medjuel had other attachments whom he kept out of sight in the desert.

Jane tried not to listen either to Sheikh Fares or to other people who would repeat such gossip.

But there were undoubtedly times when she could not be with Medjuel and when it would be quite easy for him to have another wife or another woman, which after all was what would be expected of a Bedouin.

Now it seemed that she was to be confronted by an even more insidious rival than any young and beautiful Arab girl could be.

'A replica of myself when young!'

Jane knew that at sixty-two she was still beautiful, too many men had loved her for her not to recognise the admiration and the glint of fire in masculine eyes when they looked at her.

At the same time Medjuel, younger than herself, was still a virile, handsome and attractive man.

'Supposing, just supposing,' Jane asked herself, 'he should fall in love with Vita and she with him?'

It was an idea that made her want to cry out in agony.

How could she lose Medjuel now, the dear, the adored one for whom she had turned her back on her whole past?

Somewhere in Europe she had children, friends, ex-lovers, in-laws and all the grandeur and splendour of the estate at Holkham of her grandfather, the first Earl of Leicester.

But none of it was of any consequence beside her love for Medjuel. All through the day Jane read first Vita's letter, then Isobel's and the problem of what she should do tortured her.

For one thing she could not bear Medjuel to go to war with Sheikh Shaa-lan El Hassein.

She suffered agonies every time he was engaged in one of the all too frequent desert skirmishes. That the Mezrabs were invariably victorious was not the point.

Men were wounded, some were killed and there were always casualties amongst the horses.

Jane would cry at the thought of their Arabian thoroughbreds being wounded with the sharp spears that the Bedouins used on such occasions.

'What shall I do? *What shall I do?*'

The question presented and re-presented itself until she thought she must go mad.

Late in the evening, just before sunset, one of Medjuel's men returned to say that he would not be back that night.

He had sent the messenger because he knew that otherwise she would be worried.

They had had to travel further than they had expected after the eagle's nest, which they had not yet found, and they would therefore camp and go on hunting the next day.

For the moment Jane felt with a sigh of relief that the problem of Vita could be set aside.

But then insidiously the thought came to her that Medjuel might be staying the night with another woman, if not with Ouadijid perhaps some lovely young Arab who he had taken secretly as his wife.

It was a thought that made Jane, like Vita, cry bitterly into her pillow.

*

Vita did not sleep until just before dawn when she fell into a restless slumber through sheer exhaustion.

She had not slept for long before she was aroused by the Bedouin woman coming into her tent.

"The horses are waiting for you, lady," she said in Arabic.

When Vita did not understand, she parted the flap of the tent a little so that she could see that there were a number of men outside mounted on horses and with them was Sherifa.

With an effort Vita rose from the bed, washed and let the woman help her dress.

She drank a little coffee, but she felt as if the newly-baked bread which she tried to force between her lips would choke her.

As she finished dressing, the Bedouin woman placed all her things in her valise and carried it out to the waiting horseman.

Vita adjusted her riding hat and walked into the outer tent, hoping almost against hope that the Sheikh would be there.

The tent was empty.

She stood irresolute, wondering what to do, when a Bedouin came in from where he had been waiting outside and, bowing, said in halting French,

"I – escort *m'mselle* – my name – Nokta."

"Thank you," Vita said, "but first I wish to say farewell to the Sheikh."

"Gone – riding," Nokta said making a wide gesture with his hand towards the South.

Vita knew then that the Sheikh could not bear to see her go and would not say goodbye.

Feeling helplessly that there was nothing she could do, she followed Nokta from the tent and allowed him to help her into the saddle.

Sherifa seemed pleased to see her, but that was no consolation when Vita knew that this was the last time she would ride the magnificent white mare, the last time she would ever see the tents of El Hassein.

Nokta sprang into the saddle and immediately the cavalcade of horsemen moved off.

Vita knew they were in a hurry to convey her to the Mezrabs before the heat of the day, but even so it was already very warm as the horses stretched themselves out in a gallop.

The sun was rising in the sky and after they had travelled for perhaps an hour-and-a-half Vita saw an oasis ahead and suggested that she would like to stop.

She knew that Nokta would have preferred to go on, but she felt as if every mile took her further and further away from the Sheikh and that even to stop for a few minutes would perhaps alleviate some of the agony within her breast

"I love him! *I love him*!" she murmured and knew that all she wanted out of life was to be with him, even if it meant nothing more than one small tent in the middle of the desert.

She found herself imagining what it would be like if they camped at an oasis and just stayed there.

Then she thought despairingly that, although it might be enough for her, it would never be enough for him.

She knew instinctively that he was a man born to command, a man who must lead other people, a man who would always have ideas he must put into operation, a man who could not just stagnate, however much he loved her.

She respected him for it. Equally it was a torture to know that she could not give him all he wanted and that therefore he was sending her out of his life.

'How can you do – this to me?' she whispered in her heart. 'How can you be so cruel – so unfeeling – when I love you so desperately?'

They reached the oasis and she drank from the well.

Then, when the men had quenched their thirst, they attended to the horses.

Vita sat down in the shade of a palm tree and the men, who had seated themselves too in a circle beside the well, were laughing and talking with each other.

Then without any warning, the oasis was full of horsemen!

No one had heard them come.

There had been none of the wild war cries of the *djerid*, but suddenly they were there!

Vita looked up in astonishment and then gave a little scream of fear as one of the horsemen pulled her to her feet, lifted her and put her on a mare that carried a side saddle.

Taking hold of the bridle, he dragged Vita through the palm trees to where his own horse was waiting.

In the meantime there were shouts, cries and the sound of pistol shots from the other men, who were obviously attacking the El Hasseins who had been sitting by the well.

Vita tried to look back to see what was happening, but she found herself galloping across the desert and knew from the thudding of hoofs behind her that a number of the horsemen were following.

For a moment she wondered if she had in fact been rescued by Mezrabs who had come in answer to her letter.

But when she glanced at the men who rode beside her, it seemed to her that there was no welcome on their faces and they were not smiling.

They looked grim and she felt apprehensive and afraid.

They galloped for some way before Vita was able to say in halting Arabic,

"Who are you? Where are you – taking me?"

She knew that the man she spoke to understood what she said, but he just gave her an enigmatic glance with his dark eyes and they galloped on.

They rode for what seemed to Vita to be an aeon of time, but actually could not have been more than two hours.

She knew by then that there was no chance that she was being taken to the Mezrab's camp, because by the time they reached the oasis Nokta had told her that she had already travelled half way.

The explanation must be that for some unknown reason she had been captured by another tribe, but who they could be and why they were interested in her she had no idea.

Perhaps it was just an effort to provoke the Hasseins and was nothing more explosive than the usual hostility between the Aenezes and the Shammers.

Whatever it might be it was clear that her captors had no intention of answering her questions. She was therefore forced into silence and just continued riding, thankful that they had at least provided her with a side saddle.

The mare she was mounted on did not compare with Sherifa. At the same time the Arabian thoroughbred moved so smoothly that Vita knew that she had never ridden a horse at full gallop almost as comfortably as if she was in a carriage.

She was certain that the mare was one of the five great strains of breed that the Sheikh had explained to her; perhaps an Abéyan, but she was not certain.

The Sheikh had told her the Abeyéyans were generally the most handsome breed of Arabians and there was no doubt that the bay mare, now that she could see it more easily, was extremely fine.

Once again the idea came to Vita that if only she could take back one of these thoroughbred horses to her father he would not be so angry with her.

Then she could not help wondering if indeed she would ever see home or any of her family again.

Where was she being taken? What was happening?

Although the Sheikh had called her courageous, she felt fear beginning to creep over her like a poison and she knew that she was very frightened.

Another twenty minutes' ride brought them over a hill of sand and in sight of a camp.

There were perhaps only thirty tents sheltering beneath a bare rock and, as they rode down towards it, Vita saw that there were no cattle or sheep around and was sure that the tribe was not settled here but merely resting.

It was difficult, however, to formulate any of her thoughts because she was so apprehensive of what lay ahead.

There were so many questions she wanted to ask and she only prayed that when she was brought to the Sheikh or the head of the tribe who had captured her, he would at least speak one of the languages she could understand.

The men escorting her drew up their horses abruptly with the usual flourish and the man who had first captured her at the oasis dismounted and helped her from the saddle.

Instinctively Vita shook out the skirts of her riding habit and pulled her hat a little more firmly on her head.

She knew that the man was waiting as she did so and, when finally she was ready, she lifted her chin and walked with deliberate slowness towards the tent erected on the West of the camp.

It was large and Vita felt a rich soft Persian carpet beneath her feet as she entered.

After the brilliance of the sunshine outside it took her a moment to adjust her eyes to the dim shadows of the tent.

Then she saw that, sitting at the far end of it on a red *roffe* that somehow had the appearance of a throne, was a Sheikh.

There was no mistaking the richness of his *abbas* and the authority he exuded as he waited for her to advance towards him.

He was a middle-aged man with a small beard, the black piercing eyes of the desert and a high-bridged nose.

He looked, Vita thought swiftly, like a bird of prey and she hoped that the fear that seemed to strike through her did not show itself.

"*Salam aleyk*, Miss Ashford," the Sheikh said as she drew near to him.

The Sheikh had spoken in English with the exception of the words of greeting and, as Vita dropped a small curtsey she asked,

"You know my name?"

"You are even more beautiful than I was told you were," the Sheikh replied.

There was something in the way he said it that made Vita stiffen and deem his remark an impertinence.

"I have asked you a question," she said.

"My reply really answers it," the Sheikh answered. "If you prefer me to be more explicit, let me tell you that I have brought you here to marry me!"

For a moment Vita felt that she must have misunderstood what he said.

Then in a voice hardly sounding like her own she repeated,

"To – *marry you*?"

"Perhaps first should introduce myself," the Sheikh said. "I am Fares El Meziad!"

Vita's eyes widened.

She remembered now Hedjaz speaking of Sheikh Fares El Meziad and asking if he was still pursuing her cousin Jane.

Hedjaz had then explained to her that Sheikh Fares El Meziad had coveted Sheikh Medjuel's wife ever since they were married and had pursued her relentlessly.

Holding herself even more proudly Vita said coldly,

"I have heard gossip since I have been in Syria that you were attracted by my cousin, the Honourable Jane Digby El Mezrab!"

"What you heard was correct!" the Sheikh replied, "but please seat yourself, Miss Ashford. I am sure you are in need of coffee."

There was, Vita felt, nothing to be gained by standing and she sat down on a *roffe* that the Sheikh indicated to her. It was set sideways to the one where he was seated.

There was a low table in front of it and immediately black slaves brought coffee and sweetmeats and, thinking wildly of what she must do, Vita deliberately drank a little of the coffee before she spoke again.

Sheikh Fares dismissed the slaves with a wave of his hand and then he said,

"Shall we continue our conversation?"

"If you please," Vita replied, "but I am wondering if I am not imagining the fantastic statement you have just made to me."

"Hardly fantastic," Sheikh Fares replied, "and really quite reasonable. As you have heard, I fell in love with the beautiful Jane Digby as soon as she arrived in Syria."

Vita said nothing and after a moment he went on,

"She has however consistently refused me and I was in despair until I learnt that a girl younger and even more lovely than Jane could have been at her age had been kidnapped by Sheikh Shaa-lan."

"He was sending me to the Mezrab camp," Vita answered.

"So my spies informed me," Sheikh Fares said. "I have followed your movements very carefully ever since you were carried away by the El Hasseins."

"I shall be rescued the moment Sheikh Shaa-lan hears what has happened," Vita said sharply.

Sheikh Fares smiled somewhat unpleasantly.

"He may attempt to do so," he said, "but we shall be ready for him. Moreover by the time he arrives you will be my wife."

"You really think I would marry you?" Vita asked. "My answer is of course 'no' to such a suggestion!"

"It was not an invitation but a command," the Sheikh replied. "I do not know whether you have been told of how a Bedouin woman is married?"

Vita was suddenly still.

She remembered how Signor Dira had explained to her that all the bridegroom had to do was to cut the throat of a lamb before witnesses. As soon as the blood fell to the ground the marriage ceremony was regarded as complete.

She felt herself shiver, but bravely she replied,

"I am not a Bedouin and therefore a Bedouin marriage would not be binding as far as I am concerned."

"That does not interest me," the Sheikh replied. "You would be my wife and as my wife it would be impossible for you to leave me unless I wished you to do so. We will be married, Miss Ashford, as soon as you have bathed and changed your clothes, which I am sure you will wish to do."

Vita's impulse was to defy him.

Then she thought that the only possible hope she had of escape from this incredible situation was to play for time.

She did not believe that Sheikh Fares's men would have killed all the El Hasseins who were escorting her.

They might have wounded one or two, she thought. But doubtless several of them would have ridden back to the camp and explained to the Sheikh what had happened.

'He will come for me – I know it!' Vita thought.

With deliberate slowness she finished her coffee and then forced herself to eat one of the sweetmeats.

It seemed to stick in her throat and yet she knew it would delay matters and it was something that the Bedouins would understand because the East was never in a hurry.

All the time she ate and drank Sheikh Fares was watching her and there was something in his eyes that made her afraid.

Vita was very innocent, as were all girls of her age, but she had not listened to the tempestuous drama of her cousin's life without realising that love between a man and a woman involved more than kisses.

She was not quite certain what it was, but she knew that for Sheikh Fares to touch her would be a horror beyond anything she could imagine when all she wanted was to be in the arms of the man she loved.

Finally, when she could no longer drink from an empty coffee cup, she raised her eyes to Sheikh Fares and instantly he clapped his hands and the black slaves appeared.

He gave an order in Arabic and Vita knew that he was telling them to take her to a tent which, as she had expected, was adjacent to the one they were in.

It was nearly as big and very much more impressive than the one she had been given by the El Hasseins.

Here there was a very large divan-type bed, which made her shudder at the implication and there was a low table with a looking glass on it.

The walls of the tent were hung with silks and there was the scent of incense.

The women who attended her were chattering amongst themselves and catching the word 'marriage', Vita realised that they had been told she was to be Sheikh Fares's bride.

She wondered desperately if it would be best for her to run away into the desert.

But she knew that in the soft sand she would not get far before being dragged back ignominiously by Sheikh Fares's men.

Since that would be a humiliation she could not contemplate, she meekly allowed the women to help her out of her riding clothes and she bathed in water strongly scented with rose oil.

Sheikh Fares had said that she could change her clothes and Vita wondered how this was possible as she was sure her valise would have been left behind in the oasis.

But the women brought her a robe, shapeless like theirs, but made of some thin white material thickly embroidered with silver and set with precious stones round the neck.

Vita knew that it was a bridal gown!

She debated with herself the possibility of refusing to wear it and putting on her riding clothes again.

Then she thought that there was no point in making a scene and in any case, as if the women had anticipated this might be her attitude, they had removed her clothes from the tent.

Without protest she let them help her with the white gown.

She had to admit as she looked at herself in the mirror, it was very becoming and she wondered despairingly if by any means she could make herself so unattractive that the Sheikh would not wish to marry her.

But all she could see was a perfect oval face, large eyes wide with fear and the fair hair that haloed her head and glinted in the sunlight flittering through the flap of the tent.

She took as long as possible to dress, but even so, however much she procrastinated there came a point when she had to admit that there was nothing more she could do, but she must join Sheikh Fares.

The women led her back to the big tent and Vita knew that it was not only courtesy on their part but because they had been told not to leave her.

Now Sheikh Fares was not alone, there were a number of men, all wearing embroidered *abases* and seated round on the red *roffes* with silk cushions behind them.

They were smoking their *narghilyés* and the air seemed thick with the sweet scent of tobacco mingling with the fragrance of coffee.

When Vita came into the tent, none of the men rose. They merely stared at her appreciatively and it seemed to her that there was a long pause before finally Sheikh Fares said,

"Come and sit beside me. As soon as we are ready the ceremony can begin."

"I thought it was customary for the bride to play 'hard-to-get' and to run away in fear and reluctance," Vita said icily.

She saw the amusement in his dark eyes at her retort before he replied,

"A show of maidenly modesty is expected by our people – but after the ceremony, not before it."

They were both speaking in English and, because Vita was quite certain that the other men present did not know the language, she said,

"Do you really mean to behave in this primitive and uncivilised manner?"

"I should have thought that I was being very civilised," Sheikh Fares replied. "After all, I could take you without marriage!"

"A marriage which is only a mockery as far as I am concerned," Vita asserted.

"It is an occasion for feasting," he replied, "and may I say that for me it is a very fortunate occasion. As I have said before, you are very beautiful!"

"That is not a compliment coming from you!" Vita said rudely.

He smiled again and she realised as she spoke that nothing she could say would upset or deter him.

He was supremely confident of his power over her and that he had the whip hand. There was no appeal she could make to save herself or to divert him from his chosen course.

Slowly Vita walked towards him and, when she reached him, she said quietly,

"Let me go. You know as well as I do that this will cause an immense amount of trouble not only for me but also for you!"

"There will be no trouble as far as I am concerned," Sheikh Fares replied. "You are everything that I have always desired, but which your cousin denied me. Now I shall consider myself the most fortunate man in the whole of Syria."

He was not being sarcastic and his eyes, as he glanced at her in her gown, which did not entirely conceal the curves of her body, were dark with lust.

There was in his expression something that Vita knew was very different to the fire that had been in Sheikh Shaalan's eyes when she knew that he not only desired but also loved her.

Silently she sent out a despairing call for help, a cry that came from the very depths of her soul.

'Help me! *Save me*!' she called and thought that somehow, because he loved her as she loved him, he must know how much she needed him.

Sheikh Fares put out his hand and indicated the place beside him where he wished Vita to sit.

Feeling that there was nothing else she could do, she sat down, every nerve in her body tense, aware that she was trembling, but still holding her head proudly and determined not to let the men watching her be aware of how terrified she was.

Sheikh Fares said something to them that Vita did not understand, which made them laugh, and then he snapped his fingers.

Through the wide open flap, which was pinned back to reveal the undulating desert outside, came a man carrying a small lamb.

It was still not yet noon, the sun was beating down on the sand and it was very hot.

Then, as Sheikh Fares rose to his feet, Vita knew what she must do.

It seemed almost as if someone put the idea into her head, explaining every action, every word she must speak and showed her the solution.

Sheikh Fares turned to look at her with a smile on his thick lips.

"I will now cut the throat of the lamb," he said. "Then you will be my wife!"

"It is a strange custom," Vita said slowly as she too rose. "Do I stand beside you?"

"If it pleases you," the Sheikh answered.

"I would not wish to do anything that was incorrect."

She walked beside the Sheikh across the thickly carpeted tent to where the man with the lamb was standing just inside the entrance.

As Sheikh Fares reached him, one of the slaves came forward with a long thin knife, which had a jewelled handle.

It was resting on a tray and, as Sheikh Fares put out his hand to take it, Vita was quicker.

She snatched up the knife and backing away so that she stood against the side of the tent where no one could approach her from behind and then she said,

"What is being sacrificed is not the lamb, but me! Therefore I must die!"

She held the knife by the handle and put the point against her left breast.

There was a sudden gasp and Vita knew that Sheikh Fares was for the moment paralysed into immobility.

The men on the *roffes* stopped smoking and stared.

There was a silence broken only by the pitiful bleating of the lamb.

"I mean what I say," Vita said. "Unless you give me your word of honour that this mockery of a marriage will not take place and that you will set me free, I will kill myself."

"You do not mean it," Sheikh Fares replied. "No woman as lovely as you would wish to die in such a fashion."

"I am not afraid of dying," Vita retorted, "but only of being touched by you."

Sheikh Fares took a hesitant step towards her and she raised the hand holding the knife a little as if preparing to thrust it violently into her breast.

She saw that Sheikh Fares was not only disconcerted, but was also trying to think how to trick her.

It was impossible for anyone to approach her from behind and the men on the *roffes* made no attempt to rise.

"Do you agree to set me free?" Vita asked, "or must I die?"

Still Sheikh Fares hesitated and at that moment pandemonium broke loose.

There were wild war cries which Vita had heard once before in the *djerid* and yet now they were nearer – almost at hand.

Then suddenly as she stood, the knife still poised to strike at her breast, a horse came galloping straight into the tent.

There was a man lying low over its head and she saw Sheikh Fares topple over backwards, although whether this was caused by impact of the horse or the weapon of its rider Vita had no idea.

She heard the tables crash, the coffee cups break.

Then suddenly she was swept off the ground and she knew even as two hands lifted her, whose they were.

The knife dropped from her fingers and she hid her head against a *burnouse*, uttering a cry of happiness that came from the very depths of her heart.

She thought afterwards that she must have been half unconscious with the sheer relief of knowing that she need not die and need not be married to Sheikh Fares.

Vaguely she heard shots, shouts and screams, then a strong arm held her close and the horse beneath her was galloping with the smooth unrestricted stride that she knew so well.

It was so wonderful to feel safe that it was almost impossible to move.

But with an effort Vita turned her face upwards and, as she did so, the Sheikh's mouth came down on hers and she knew as his lips held her captive that nothing else in the world mattered except him.

Chapter Seven

The kiss was more wonderful, more perfect than anything Vita had known before.

She felt as if she surrendered her whole self to the Sheikh and he took her masterfully for his own.

When finally he raised his head, she made a little murmur of happiness and hid her face against him.

He drew his horse to a standstill.

"My darling! My sweet! Are you all right?"

"I was – about to – kill myself," she answered, "because he – intended to – marry me and I could not let him – touch me."

"I thought that was what was happening when I saw the lamb."

She heard the anger in his voice.

His arms tightened around her as if he could not bear to think of what she had passed through.

"How did you – find me in time?" she asked.

It was difficult to ask the question because her heart was singing with joy at being close to him and she knew that the answer was unimportant now that he was there.

"When you left," the Sheikh answered, "I grew uneasy in case you should encounter the Mezrabs coming to fight us and they should shoot at my men, not realising that you were with them. So collecting a number of my horsemen I followed you, determined to keep out of sight, but ensuring your safety."

"I am glad – so very – glad!" Vita murmured. "I called for you – desperately to – save me. I felt somehow you would – know I was in danger."

"I did know, but I did not realise that the Sheikh's men had found you at the oasis or inflicted such damage on the members of the tribe until I saw far in the distance the Meziads galloping away with you.

"Then you went to the oasis?" Vita asked.

The Sheikh's lips tightened.

"Two of my men were dead and two horses badly speared. Sheikh Fares will pay highly for that!"

"And then you came after – me.

"By the time I had seen to my men you were out of sight and I was terrified I would not be able to find Sheikh Fares's camp."

"But you *did* – find me!" she said softly.

He bent his head and found her lips again and she thought that, if she had not been afraid of death when she had held the knife against her breast, it would be easy to die now from sheer happiness.

The Sheikh's lips only left hers when he saw horsemen approaching and knew it was his men coming from the Meziads' tents.

They were galloping wildly and, as they drew near, Vita could see the expression of satisfaction in their sparkling eyes and wide smiles.

Their saddles were loaded with loot, damasks, brocades, weapons and jewels.

As they drew up alongside the Sheikh, they told him excitedly what had happened in such rapid Arabic that Vita could not follow it.

But it was easy to understand their elation, and she knew that, having taken the camp by surprise, as Sheikh Fares had not expected them for many hours, they had made the most of it.

The Sheikh gave an order and they set off once again at a gallop.

"Where are we going?" Vita asked.

"To Damascus!"

"To Damascus?" she repeated in surprise.

"I am handing you over to the British Consul," he said. "I cannot trust you any further in the desert!"

She looked at him and he asked with a smile,

"Will you find it very uncomfortable to travel in my arms as you are now? As it happens, Damascus is less than ten miles away. It will not take so long."

"You know I want to be – close to – you," Vita answered.

At the same time her heart dropped.

She knew without his having to put it into words that he intended to leave her in Damascus.

When he had ensured her safety, he would disappear back into the desert and once again there would be the heartbreak of parting.

But she told herself that to be close to him as she was now was something she had not expected and the wonder of it must not be spoilt by the misery that lay ahead.

Charles had said that love was a pain that struck through the whole body and mind until one could hardly bear it another moment.

"Then suddenly," he said, "it is a rapture that sweeps one up into the sky and one knows that, after all, the pain is worth it."

"It will be worth this moment of rapture," Vita reassured herself.

At the same time once again she shrank from the thought of leaving the Sheikh as if it was a bleeding wound within her heart.

"My darling," he murmured and a thrill ran through her at his words.

The Sheikh felt her quiver and he pulled her almost roughly closer to him.

"My precious life, if that devil had hurt you I would have killed him."

Vita thrilled again at the violence in his voice.

"I am safe with you," she whispered.

She was in fact quite comfortable.

The Sheikh was riding on the soft cushion that served as a saddle for the Bedouins. He was without stirrups and there was only a halter round his horse's nose.

But he had complete control over the magnificent black stallion and Vita knew that it was part of his character that he should ride a stallion when it was customary for the Bedouins to use only mares for riding.

As they journeyed on, Vita was willing it that they would never reach Damascus.

If only, she wished, she could travel on for ever, held in the Sheikh's arms, conscious of his love and protection.

She knew that she was safer with him than she had ever been in her whole life.

It seemed to her that without him the world would be a very terrifying place and that she would be afraid, not only physically as she had been of Sheikh Fares, but mentally as she feared and abhorred Lord Bantham.

As if he knew what she was thinking, the Sheikh looked down at her and said,

"Do not suffer, my precious. You must tell yourself it is *Insha'Allah* and perhaps one day we will find each other again."

"One day can be very far – away," Vita replied, "I want you now – always – as we are at this moment."

She heard him draw in his breath and knew that he felt the same.

When later the domes and minarets of Damascus loomed in front of them, she thought despairingly that there was nothing more to say.

Now Damascus was not '*Sham Sherif*', 'The Holy or Blessed', but was to her the 'City of the Damned' because there she must part from the man she loved.

As they drew nearer, it was to hear the bleat of the lambs and the lowing of the cattle grazing around the City and to see the green of its gardens, which surrounded it like the waters of a lake.

But soon – so soon that time seemed to have accelerated unfairly, they had passed through the City gate.

Moving through the narrow picturesque streets, they made their way into the great square with its marble pavement, the fountains playing, shaded by orange, lemon and pomegranate trees.

The Sheikh rode ahead proudly and imperiously, Vita in his arms.

His horsemen followed behind until he stood in front of a large building with the Union Jack hanging limply in the hot sunshine.

The sentries in their red uniforms showed it to be the British Consulate.

The Sheikh drew his horse to a standstill. Vita looked up at him and saw the pain in his dark eyes.

"Why must we do – this?" she whispered. "Let me – stay with – you at least a little longer."

She saw how deeply her pleading voice affected him, but without answering her he gently lifted her down onto the ground and swung himself from the stallion's back.

One of his tribe hurried forward to take the halter and the Sheikh drew Vita through the wrought iron gate of the Consulate and they moved together towards the front door.

She could not help thinking how strange they must appear, the Sheikh in his robes, herself wearing the glittering embroidered gown the Meziad women had dressed her.

But appearances were of no consequence at the moment.

She was conscious only of the agony within herself, knowing that in a few moments the Sheikh would leave her for ever.

She could read his thoughts and knew that he intended to hand her over to Captain Richard Burton, and then he and his followers would disappear into the desert and she would never see them again.

She had appealed to him and failed, and now there was nothing she could do but try to behave with dignity when all she wanted was to burst into tears and cling onto him convulsively.

A servant was at the door and the Sheikh said authoritatively,

"Kindly inform His Excellency that Miss Vita Ashford is here!"

The man hurried across the hall to open a door and disappear behind it.

There was only a moment's pause before he reappeared holding the door open to invite them to enter.

Vita glanced up at the Sheikh, but he looked away from her and she knew by the tightness of his lips and the hard line of his jaw that he was suffering as she was.

Without a word she walked a little ahead of him across the hall and through the door the servant had opened.

She found herself in a large room with windows looking out onto a flower-filled garden.

It was cool from the *punkah* moving overhead and she saw that Captain Richard Burton was with two men.

When she appeared, he stared at her with searching dark eyes, looking, she thought, more like a tiger than he had the last time she had seen him.

Then he exclaimed with a note of astonishment in his voice,

"It really is Vita Ashford! Where in the name of Allah have you come from?"

"I have brought her back to Your Excellency," the Sheikh said.

Richard Burton came forward to clasp Vita's hand in his.

"We have been deeply worried about you," he said.

She found it impossible to speak.

Then Captain Burton held out his hand to the Sheikh.

"We heard that she was with you, Sheikh Shaa-lan," he said, "She has been kept safe?"

The two men's eyes met and there was a question in Richard Burton's, which the Sheikh answered quietly,

"Completely safe, Your Excellency!"

Captain Burton would have spoken again, but one of the men who had been standing by the window exclaimed,

"Manuel! It is Manuel, is it not?"

The Sheikh turned his head and Vita also looked at a tall, handsome young man, exquisitely dressed in the very latest fashion and accompanied by an older man with grey hair.

There was a moment's pause and Vita realised that the man who had asked the question had spoken in Spanish.

The Sheikh replied in the same language,

"Jaime! What are you doing here?"

"Looking for you!" was his answer, "and the devil of a job it has been! Don Ricardo and I thought we would have to search the whole world before we found you!"

He paused to hold out both his hands and clasp the Sheikh's as he added fervently,

"Thank God you are here and we need go no further! Oh, Manuel, I am glad to see you!"

It seemed to be difficult for the Sheikh to find words and the young man went on with a glance at the man who had stood beside him,

"You remember Don Ricardo Savedra?"

"Of course I do!" the Sheikh said, holding out his hand. "You have looked after the family estates at Valdepeñas ever since I can remember!"

"Which I am still doing," Don Ricardo answered, "and which is why I am so thankful to have found Your Grace!"

Vita saw that the Sheikh stiffened. There was something rigid about his body.

"It is true!" the young man called Jaime said. "Your father is dead. That is why we had to find you."

"But Alfonso – " the Sheikh ejaculated.

"Your older brother was killed two years ago," Don Ricardo explained. "We have been trying to find you ever since."

"I can hardly believe it," the Sheikh said almost beneath his breath.

"Are you telling me that the lost Spaniard we have been discussing and about whom you questioned me, is in fact Sheikh Shaa-lan El Hassein?" Captain Burton interposed.

"On the contrary, Your Excellency," Don Ricardo replied. "His name is Don Manuel de Canas y Garia, the Duke of Valdepeñas.

Vita gave a little gasp and as she did so the Sheikh turned towards her and took her hand in his.

"The news could not have reached me at a more opportune moment!" he said.

He looked at Richard Burton.

"I should be grateful, Your Excellency, if you would arrange for my marriage to take place to Miss Vita Ashford before we leave together for Spain!"

Vita felt his fingers tighten on hers until they were painful.

Then, as she looked up at him and the whole room seemed to be filled with sunshine, she heard Captain Burton say to her,

"Is it your wish – to be married to this man?"

"I want it more than anything in the whole world!" she answered.

There was no mistaking the radiance that transformed her face into something so exquisitely beautiful that all four men stared at her as if they were dazzled by her loveliness,

"I daresay I shall get into trouble if I allow such a precipitate marriage," Captain Burton said with a smile, "but one more injudicious action will make little difference to the sum total of my indiscretions!"

The Sheikh bowed his head.

"I thank Your Excellency!"

*

It was late in the evening when Vita stood at the window and looked out over the square, shining with silver from the light of the moon, which gave the City a strange ethereal appearance as if it was merely a figment of a dream.

She could hardly believe that she was not really dreaming and that she would not awaken to find herself travelling back alone to Naples to where a highly displeased Lady Crowen would be awaiting her.

It had been typical of the man she had married, she thought, that he had arranged matters so skilfully that everything had seemed to happen smoothly and predictably as if it was part of an inescapable Fate.

First he had insisted that she should rest, and Captain Burton had offered them a suite of rooms in the Consulate that was kept for important visitors to Damascus.

Vita was relieved that she did not have to go to the Burtons' house in the Kurd village where she knew she would have to endure innumerable questions from Mrs. Burton and try to find adequate answers to them.

Instead she found herself in a cool high-ceilinged bedroom in which, to her great relief, she found her own valise.

The Sheikh with his usual efficiency had rescued it from the oasis when he had found his followers after the Meziads had surprised them.

Because he had ordered Vita to rest and she wanted to obey him, she had not wasted time but taken off the elaborate embroidered wedding gown she had been dressed in by Sheikh Fares's women.

She put on one of her thin nightgowns and got into the big low divan bed.

It was draped with white muslin and the cover was embroidered with Arabic signs.

She fell asleep immediately and when she awoke in the cool of the evening and the sun was sinking, she found that everything had been planned down to the last detail.

It was sad, she thought, after she had bathed and dressed, to have nothing more elaborate to wear than the one evening gown she had brought with her to Damascus.

It was indeed, because she was a *debutante*, white, but it was not very elaborate and she was afraid that the Sheikh, for it was difficult for her to think of him by any other name, would not admire her in it.

So she had in fact been glad of Isobel Burton.

Mrs. Burton had arrived from her house bubbling over with excitement at the idea of a wedding and bringing with her the Brussels lace veil in which she had been married herself.

It was too late in the year for orange blossoms, but the clever fingers of Arab women contrived a wreath of small roses and other white flowers to match the bouquet Vita was to hold in her hand.

When she was dressed, she looked so lovely that, as she came down the stairs to where the British Consul, the Sheikh and his Spanish friends were waiting, the men drew in their breath as if she was some spiritual being from another world.

The expression on the Sheikh's face made Vita's heart start beating wildly and, when their eyes met and were held by some inescapable magic, she felt as if he kissed her.

They all proceeded to the Catholic Church where Vita was to be married.

Isobel Burton was ecstatic because, being a Catholic herself, nothing, she told Vita, could please her more than that she should be married to one.

The Service was very short, but very beautiful.

The small Church had been filled with flowers and Vita knew that the Sheikh had arranged for them.

It was almost difficult for her to recognise him, for he was dressed not in the Bedouin robes she had always seen him in but as a Spanish gentleman.

While she guessed that he had borrowed his clothes from his relative, Don Jaime, she thought that they made him even more handsome and more outstanding than he had looked as an Arab.

At the same time she felt somehow a new shyness when she was with him.

She knew it was because he had now become part of her world, the world she had left behind when she entered the desert.

There she had been part of his, but now they met on an equal footing, a man and a woman who were both European and both had a long line of antecedents in common.

As they made their responses in the beautiful Latin phrases that had echoed down the centuries, Vita prayed in her heart that she could make the man she married forget the bitterness and the hatred that had consumed him for so many years.

Perhaps, she thought, it would be difficult for him to re-adjust himself to his old life, but she was sure that she could help him.

There might be many obstacles ahead, but none that could not be overcome by love.

She knew that her love for him and his for her had nothing to do with the ordinary world of mundane affairs, but came from God.

'Our religions may be different,' Vita told herself, 'but our God is the same and if it will make him happy I will become a Catholic.'

As she thought of it, she was sure that all Gods were the same.

All men sought Him in some form or another and whether they ultimately reached the Heaven of the Christians, the Paradise of the Mohammedans or the Nirvana of the Buddhists, they all sought the love that made mankind part of the Divine.

"I love you! *I love you*!" Vita wanted to shout as the Sheikh put the ring on her finger.

'God, make our love perfect!' she prayed as the Priest blessed them.

They had gone back to the Consulate after the marriage.

There was a dinner party where the food was delicious and the conversation brilliant, but Vita found it hard to listen to it.

All she could think of was the man at her side, the man she now belonged to.

She had no idea what she ate or drank.

She only knew that everything seemed to be in a golden haze and, when finally Captain and Mrs. Burton had left for their house outside Damascus, she went up to her room knowing that this was the moment she had been waiting for.

Nothing else had been of any consequence.

She allowed a maid to help her undress and then she slipped on a thin white negligée over her nightgown and stood at the window.

The room was in darkness, the light came only from outside.

The beauty of the moonlight in the starlit sky seemed part of the beauty in her heart and, when she heard the door open, she did not turn round, she only waited.

He came across the room to stand beside her at the window and she knew without moving her head that he was looking not at the moonlight, but at her.

"Are you real?" he asked after a moment with a deep note in his voice that always moved her.

She turned her eyes towards his.

"I am your – wife!"

"I can hardly believe it!" he replied. "Even now I find myself waiting for the pain that was like a mortal blow when I knew that I must send you away and that I might never see you again."

"And – now? "

"Now I am grateful and thankful beyond words," he answered. "Can it really be true that anything so exquisite and so lovely can be mine for ever?"

She did not answer and after a moment he said fiercely,

"And I mean *for ever*! I will never let you go, my darling! I will never lose you! If ever you try to behave as your cousin has done, I swear I will kill you!"

Vita was not afraid of the violence in his voice.

"I think that everything that happened in Cousin Jane's life was because she was seeking – love," she said. "If she had been able to marry the man she loved when she was my age, then she would have been as happy as I am in knowing that she had found what every woman seeks – the man she belongs to."

"I am not concerned with your cousin but with you. Do you love me?"

"You know I – do."

"Say it, tell me, make me sure that there can be no other man in your life."

"I love you and – you are the – only man in the – world."

"If you even so much as glance at another, I will bring you back here to make you a Bedouin wife and I will beat you into submission!"

Vita smiled, at the same time the fierce jealousy in his voice thrilled her,

"There will – never be anyone but – you."

"I shall be jealous to the point of madness – autocratic, impatient, intolerant and perhaps at times cruel to you."

"I shall – still love – you."

"Can you be certain?"

"I am yours!" Vita answered. "I was yours from the moment you first – kissed me. I knew – then that I was a – part of – you."

He still did not touch her but looked down into her face before he exclaimed,

"You are so beautiful! So incredibly, indescribably beautiful!"

His voice sharpened as he added,

"There is a great deal to be said for a Bedouin marriage where the woman is utterly subservient to her husband, where she has no thoughts or existence apart from him."

"I am prepared to be as you – wish me to – be," Vita said. "In the language of the Bedouins – I am at your – feet!"

"If that was true," he replied, "I should not be so apprehensive of the agonies I must suffer because of your irresistible face. But you are not at my feet, my precious one, you are in a shrine in my heart where I will worship you now and for Eternity. At the same time I want you and need you as a woman!"

There was a raw note in his voice that made Vita want to throw herself into his arms and yet some instinct told her that there were things that must be said between them before he touched her.

Again as if he knew her thoughts the Sheikh said almost impatiently,

"I have been busy arranging that we can leave tomorrow. We will stop at Naples on our way to Spain so that you can pick up your luggage and make your peace with your chaperone."

He saw that Vita was not particularly interested and he went on,

"When we reach Spain, there are many things I will give you to prove my love, but I also have a wedding present to give you here, which I think will please you."

"What is it?" Vita asked.

"I have instructed Nokta, who fortunately was unhurt in the skirmish at the oasis, to return to the camp with a letter of explanation for Hedjaz. I have told him that there need be no fighting between the Medjuels and Hasseins."

"I am so glad," Vita cried.

"I have also told him," he went on, "to bring three horses back with him to Damascus as soon as possible."

He paused to say with a smile,

"Two I will send to your father as a peace offering! The third, Sherifa, will be dispatched to you in Spain!"

Vita gave a little cry.

"You could give me nothing I want more! Thank you! Oh, my darling wonderful husband, thank you – more than I can say!"

Now, because she could wait no longer, she reached out towards him and he pulled her into his arms.

As her fair head fell back against his shoulder, he looked down at her in the moonlight.

"I adore you!" he said passionately. "I worship you and the ground you walk on. But I need you as a man has never needed a woman before! I want above all else to arouse the fire in you that burns in me, a fire so primitive and uncivilised, my precious, that I am afraid I may frighten you."

There was a deep pulsating note in his voice that Vita had not heard before.

"You could never – frighten me," she whispered. "Make me – love you the way you – want me to."

She lifted her lips to his as she spoke and his mouth came down on hers.

She felt the fire and felt herself respond to it.

It was, as he had said, wild and primitive – the fire of love. Strong and tempestuous – it was a flame that consumed them both and carried them away from the world up into the starlit sky.

The Sheikh held Vita so close that she knew she was already a part of him.

Then he drew her closer and closer still until their hearts were beating against each other arid she could no longer think but only feel herself burning with her love and her need for him.

He raised his head.

"This is Fate," he said. "This is '*Insha'Allah*', my lovely darling, and there is no escape for either of us."

His lips possessed hers.

As her arms went round his neck, he lifted her up and carried her away into the shadows.

OTHER BOOKS IN THIS SERIES

The Barbara Cartland Eternal Collection is the unique opportunity to collect all five hundred of the timeless beautiful romantic novels written by the world's most celebrated and enduring romantic author.

Named the Eternal Collection because Barbara's inspiring stories of pure love, just the same as love itself, the books will be published on the internet at the rate of four titles per month until all five hundred are available.

The Eternal Collection, classic pure romance available worldwide for all time.

1. Elizabethan Lover
2. The Little Pretender
3. A Ghost in Monte Carlo
4. A Duel of Hearts
5. The Saint and the Sinner
6. The Penniless Peer
7. The Proud Princess
8. The Dare-Devil Duke
9. Diona and a Dalmatian
10. A Shaft of Sunlight
11. Lies for Love
12. Love and Lucia
13. Love and the Loathsome Leopard
14. Beauty or Brains
15. The Temptation of Torilla
16. The Goddess and the Gaiety Girl
17. Fragrant Flower
18. Look, Listen and Love
19. The Duke and the Preacher's Daughter
20. A Kiss For The King
21. The Mysterious Maid-Servant
22. Lucky Logan Finds Love
23. The Wings of Ecstasy
24. Mission to Monte Carlo
25. Revenge of the Heart
26. The Unbreakable Spell
27. Never Laugh at Love
28. Bride to a Brigand
29. Lucifer and the Angel
30. Journey to a Star
31. Solita and the Spies
32. The Chieftain without a Heart
33. No Escape from Love
34. Dollars for the Duke
35. Pure and Untouched
36. Secrets
37. Fire in the Blood
38. Love, Lies and Marriage
39. The Ghost who fell in love
40. Hungry for Love
41. The wild cry of love
42. The blue eyed witch
43. The Punishment of a Vixen
44. The Secret of the Glen
45. Bride to The King
46. For All Eternity
47. A King inLove

48. A Marriage Made in Heaven
49. Who Can Deny Love?
50. Riding to The Moon
51. Wish for Love
52. Dancing on a Rainbow
53. Gypsy Magic
54. Love in the Clouds
55. Count the Stars
56. White Lilac
57. Too Precious to Lose
58. The Devil Defeated
59. An Angel Runs Away
60. The Duchess Disappeared
61. The Pretty Horse-breakers
62. The Prisoner of Love
63. Ola and the Sea Wolf
64. The Castle made for Love
65. A Heart is Stolen
66. The Love Pirate
67. As Eagles Fly
68. The Magic of Love
69. Love Leaves at Midnight
70. A Witch's Spell
71. Love Comes West
72. The Impetuous Duchess
73. A Tangled Web
74. Love Lifts the Curse
75. Saved By A Saint
76. Love is Dangerous
77. The Poor Governess
78. The Peril and the Prince
79. A Very Unusual Wife
80. Say Yes Samantha
81. Punished with love
82. A Royal Rebuke
83. The Husband Hunters
84. Signpost To Love
85. Love Forbidden
86. Gift of the Gods
87. The Outrageous Lady
88. The Slaves of Love
89. The Disgraceful Duke
90. The Unwanted Wedding
91. Lord Ravenscar's Revenge
92. From Hate to Love
93. A Very Naughty Angel
94. The Innocent Imposter
95. A Rebel Princess
96. A Wish Come True
97. Haunted
98. Passions In The Sand

Made in the USA
Lexington, KY
20 February 2018